MIDNIGHT LOVE

the dance between genres

a short story collection of

erotic encounters, inspiration,

drama and more

About the Author

Born in The Town of Cortland (Peekskill Hospital) in 1972, her parents the late Mr. Alvin Draper and Ms. Audrey Scott relocated to Yonkers NY, where she resided until 1992 then relocated to Boston, MA. A single mother of three, MzSHE penned the first edition of MIDNIGHT LOVE via eBook in 2015, which became a bestseller on Amazon in Poetic Erotica.

Shortly after the book released, she suffered the devastating loss of her beloved Mother. It was not an easy decision, but she pulled the book from the market due to the unbearable grief. MzSHE felt it was unfair to be non-responsive to the readers. After taking the time to grieve, she came back stronger than ever with alternative endings, added stories and overall greatness in this version that tops the first. The resolve and determination that MzSHE has displayed is a force to be reckoned with! The resolve and determination she has displayed is a force to be reckoned with! She is proof that it is never too late to go after your dreams. Please enjoy the read.

§

To Write to the Author

If you wish to contact the author about any upcoming events, please send an email to officialauthor-mzshe42@gmail.com. You can also follow her on *Facebook* www.facebook.com/officialMzShe and *Instagram* @MzShe-She

From the Author

Thank you for taking the time to read my work! I have to admit in advance, some of the stories are a bit of a teaser, forgive me (smile). I want you to see the scenery, hear the music, feel the wind and the warm rays of sun as you read. I hope to awaken your passion and put your fears to sleep. I would greatly appreciate hearing about how you enjoyed the book, how it has helped you, or feedback, questions or suggestions!

I will do my best to respond, but cannot guarantee a turn-around time. I was inspired to begin again by the words of my beloved mother before she was born into eternity; *"I am so proud of you, keep reaching past the stars!"* How could I not honor her? So, I ask that you help make becoming a #1 bestseller a dream come true again. You have not only purchased words on a page, but an EXPERIENCE! Peace and Many Blessings, MzSHE

Library of Congress Cataloging-in-Publication Data is on file
Name: MzSHE
Title: MIDNIGHT LOVE: the dance between genres / by MzSHE
US Distribution

Book design by: MzSHE
Cover design by: MzSHE
Logo design by: MzSHE

Dedicated to my beloved Mother, my Universe, my first Love. She told me a few things I hold close to me:

1. Don't worry about people talking about you, be concerned when they are not because you must be slippin'
2. I am very proud of you! Keep moving forward and don't worry so much about what other people think! You are strong, and I always knew this, even from your birth. You can do anything you set out to!
3. Don't bother me during my stories! LOL (I always did on purpose)
4. I LOVE YOU

I will miss your calls, and calling you at God-awful hours. I will do my best to continue to make you proud. I LOVE YOU MORE.

Table of Contents

Adanna Speaks...SHHH Not a Word

Hey baby
I don't want you to say a word
Just listen
Art of Noise Moments in Love plays in
the background
Every time I think of out verbal en-
counters
My SHE awakens
The baritone in your voice commands
Pink Panther pays attention
SHE is obedient to her master
SHE begins to purr
Craving to hear your instruction
But alas, you are not here
So I must pull them from our previous
dialect
MMMMMMM
Your voice vibrates my mind
Travels down my spine
OOOH YES
That's the spot
Pink Panther begins to swell
My clit oh so sensitive to touch
She wants to come out to play
But your warm mouth
Your thick tongue
Isn't here to greet her
SHE begins to shout obscenities through
her throbbing
Dripping
Pulsating
She needs to release
BREATHING SHALLOW
BITING MY LIP

I can't contain the river of sweetness
rising
The waves of ecstasy crashing against
my fingers
My blush colored opening like a vortex
Yearning to suck you in
AND
Swallow you whole
OH BABY
I can feel the head moving along my
sugar walls
I writhe
My vibrator humming feverishly
Massaging my pearl
SHE is so hard
I sway to my rhythm
Intoxicated
Feeling lascivious
I'm so high
The mental image of you
Brings forth
EROTIC THOUGHTS
Your tongue thick
I love it when you greedily stare
Slanting your eyes
Biting your bottom lip
Eyebrow raised
You're contemplating
Where to begin
Head slightly tilted to the right
You're studying me
OH HONEY
Put your hands all over my body
Art of Noise still serenades in the
background
The part of the song that screams NOW
is on

My fingers cramping
Exploring
Gasping
Breathless
I LET OUT A PRIMAL SCREAM
BODY JERKS
LEGS QUIVER
ABDOMEN TIGHT
SHE SHOOTS
PROJECTILE
SHEETS SOAKED
EYES ROLLING TO THE BACK OF MY HEAD
FACE CONTORTED
OOOOOH
Gratification achieved
Self-indulgence
Always a pleasure
While licking my fingers
I gently allow them
To glide along my tongue
Pushing my bottom lip down ever so
slightly
This meal is too much for just one
Shorten the distance
Include me in your life
Let us create something so powerful
We will have our own constellation
Among the stars
CLICK

§

Warm Summer Stroll

Seth sat on his sofa staring at the phone. A whirlwind of emotions came flooding in at once. He was shocked, confused, a little peeved because she left him hanging, literally! The D swollen, rock solid, veins popped and nuts full of cum that needs to be released is the current situation. However, once he had a moment to think, he had to chuckle and say to himself: "Adanna is good; she no longer wants the empty talk." Time for some action, he listened, and received the message clearly.

After he finished what she had started (hell he wasn't about to go to bed like that) he immediately went online to book her ticket. There was no way he was going to take the chance of her leaving him. There is something about this woman that has me captivated he thought to himself. He has grown tired of the dating scene. Although they had never met, he had already begun to develop feelings for her. He wondered if she held anything in her heart for him as well. Only one way to find out…

When she stepped off the plane, it was as if he could feel her presence. When she entered the airport, his eyes caught hers, stunning and graceful she is. Paralyzed in place, speechless and barely breathing he had to muster the strength to get to her. Never had he felt such passion and awe in his life. He had absolutely no regrets bringing her to him. Once he reached her, the embrace was so sensual it caused many to stare in envy.

He decided to take her on a romantic stroll through the park he frequented on his daily runs. Now that he had her in his arms, he realized he never stopped to take in the beauty the park contained. Quite possibly, it was because he had no one in his life that he wanted to share the ambiance with. That is, until now…

Seth and I were strolling along on this warm summer night. Our hands interlocked, slightly rocking back and forth as we ventured into the dimly lit park. We found a spot to rest my weary feet under a dimly lit light. With the setting perfect, romantic dialect between lovers shall begin. Before I sat, he checked to be sure the seat was clear of any and all debris, a perfect gentleman. I sat down, but apparently too far away from him. He told me to come closer, he needed to feel me. When I breathed out, he could breathe me in. I did so without delay or question.

He put his hand on the small of my back. I quivered, my pussy pulsated, and my sweet nectar began to trickle. Damn, already ignited! He said he wanted to share a thought with me, but this particular thought had to fall directly into my ear. No one else could hear these thoughts, too precious to share even with the creatures of the night. So I put my hand on his firm thigh, leaned into him, slightly tilting my head so this tantalizing sweet honey that dripped from his mouth would rest in my ear. Not wanting to spill one drop, I listened.

I wanted his breath on my neck and ear. I wanted his scent to embed itself into my very being, into my soul. His words were like lyrical liquor to me, and I was intoxicated from them. His voice resounded through me, vibrations down my body. With every word, my spine was as if it was a xylophone, musical. My forbidden, exotic succulent fruit engorged. If he were to bite in, oh baby the juice would burst forth in his mouth like a summer peach. I was ready to take him into me!

As he spoke to me ever so softly, full of passion, he massaged my thigh. Mutha fucka! He teased me, never going to the height of my pink heaven letting off intense heat at this point. I was shifting back and forth, discreetly massaging myself with a steady rhythm, flexing my Kegel muscles. Well, I thought it was discreetly. I was so lost in my own thoughts; I didn't realize he stopped talking.

Seth knew exactly what I needed; he knew my pudenda was ripe. He took out his phone and played Pandora. Silk came on, serenading "let me lick you up and down, till you say stop." (fuck if that happens)! Immediately he began to move his hand up my thigh, slowly and methodically working his way to my awaiting pussy, massaging me all the way. The heat was intense, no longer warm and inviting. I spread my legs, slouched down into his hands, allowing him access to the treasure room; he knew he held the key. This chocolate son of a bitch!

He never missed a beat. Speaking once again, he put his breath on my neck with precision. He exhaled my name "Adanna," and I was gone! He slipped his fingers inside me, now having full access to the river of nectar that had overflowed its bank. He slid my black satin with red laced thongs (purposely worn) aside and gently placed two of his fingers inside me. GASP! He withdrew them to taste me, while looking me directly in my eyes. THAT'S THAT SHIT RIGHT THERE!

He sucked my sweetness off his fingers like he just finished a good meal. Hell, he did! He let out a long, deep MMMMM…DELICIOUS, never breaking his gaze. He put his fingers back into their rightful place, another gasp. With two fingers in my pussy, he used that long ass thumb to massage my swollen pearl. I was just dizzy from the intense passion, breathing deeply, cooing softly. He was killing me with his touch, melting me with his words, I was gone!

He spread my pussy lips with his fingers, and massaged my breasts with the other hand. He worked a smooth, circular rhythm with my clit while the other fingers were working me, in and out. I gripped his dick through his linen pants, and he was throbbing with pleasure for me. He was hard as marble. Large enough; I declared it a pillar in his own right. GOT DAMN! Pre cum seeped through his clothing, letting me know he was ready to explode! I unzipped his pants to truly feel the magnificent specimen before me, and he did not disappoint.

The passion between us was explosive! Anyone who dared to venture close would burst into flames from the intense heat! We began to sweat; we were both throbbing, and both longing to know how each other felt inside. Him inside of me enveloping his dick with the warmth of my ignited pussy. I massaged him, tracing the veins on his dick that popped, loving the feeling of him in my hands. I wanted to put his dick in my mouth, devouring every bit of him, deep throat his fine ass.

Seth began to moan and held me with the tightest grip; he was sending me over the edge! Nothing is hotter than a man who isn't afraid to let you know how much you are freaking him! He pulled me to his soft, pillow like lips and passionately kissed me. Shit, he tried to lick my tonsils! Giving me as much tongue as he could, I sucked it like a pro. Secretly, I longed to put my mouth on his other muscle. In due time, I told myself.

He continued to explore my pussy like he was curious about her make-up. He said "Adanna, how could you taste so good? How could my pussy be so incredibly tight, yet so fuckin wet?" Thick girls have that snap back (wink). As I writhed to euphoric heights, he never let up. His thumb moving at lightning speed on my clit, finger fuckin my pussy, his other fingers exploring my anus, I was about to explode! He brought me to the brink of destruction, the walls had to collapse, and the sea of my sweetness had to burst forth!

Not being able to hold back the orgasm he was bringing on any longer, my breathing became quick with intensity. I let the breath out of my lungs. It was the level of a last gasp of a dying person, and there it was, an orgasm of the likes the world has never seen! I soaked his fingers, I shook and trembled. My face; just as ugly with a satisfied scowl. I cursed his very existence, in a good way though. Disorientated, shocked and just fuckin impressed!

He once again sucked my essence off each finger, holding my gaze, burning straight through my soul. However, he was not done with me yet. He stood up in front of me and fastened his pants. Never taking his eyes from mine, they were still burrowing deep within mine. He said he loved the twinkle in my eyes. That twinkle was like the North Star, able to lead him home. He began praising the woman I am, the beauty he loved gazing at, and I could do nothing more than blush. I absorbed it all!

Before I could say WTF, he laid me down and told me to open up for him. I obeyed once again without hesitation. He put his hands underneath me to hold my ass up, so he could dive deep within my pussy; he wanted to finish the meal he sampled earlier off his fingers. Tha fuck?! He put his face into my smoking hot pussy. Breathless! The fire he began in me would be quenched!

He licked my clit with just the right amount of pressure. The tongue is the strongest muscle in the body, and he was going to show me why! I threw my head back as I once again let out all the air in my lungs, he took my breath away! Then he blew on my pussy, and took my SHE into his mouth. He used his bottom lip to stimulate the entrance to desire. He then flicked my clit with his tongue. When he licked, he kept his tongue on her the whole time, alternating the level of pressure on my shit. I swear I drew some blood biting the shit out of my lip!

Damn him! He was fucking me up and sending me to new heights of pure ecstasy, and I loved every minute of it! He licked, sucked and pleasured until he brought forth another earth shattering orgasm! When my river of nectar burst its bank, I let out a high-pitched OOOOHHH SETH! YES BABY! As my body jerked and began to quiver under his fucking tongue, he called out my name. ADANNA! I GOT YOU BABY! He got his fill as he drank every drop of my sweet sticky, not willing to spill one drop. Just then, Seth promised to make me feel loved every time.

I was so caught up in my earth shattering orgasm that I missed what he just said. What I did hear was this; "Adanna, you are to never just cum for me, but you are and will be required to shake under me EVERY time! I will not stop until you are completely, and utterly satisfied with the foreplay that is my pleasure to give. You are a magnificent woman, and it will be my sworn duty to ensure you know this. If you will have me, you will never lack admiration, and never question if I carry you with me. I am a busy man, just like you are a busy woman. I am impressed by the way you hold your own. However, you will no longer have to carry the world on those delicate shoulders."

I am now focused on the words dripping from his mouth. So sweet and delectable, I swear I could taste them. I am just stunned, just as he was when we first met, speechless. I am not a potential partner to him; he has made up his mind! I am not some penny candy to him, but his dime piece. Wait correction. Men don't carry change. He has no interest in a broken dollar. No interest in dating others, no fragments. Seth then said something that made me sit up and pay attention. He stated in a rather matter of fact way that I am special to him, and he promised to make me feel loved every time. LOVED?

Pandora's Box

From the sweat of our bodies
We produced an elixir
Specially made for us
The GODS wish they could have a taste
My skin
Kiss it
Lick it
Pandora's Box is locked
Become intoxicated from the salty flavor
Then suck the sweetness from Pink Panther
Slurp
Smack your lips
Then breathe on my other pair
Tease
Taunt
Enjoy her
SHE can't get enough of you
Pandora's Box still locked
What you give
Erotic love
Put that ice in your mouth
Let it melt
Drip drip
On top of my clit
My body jerks

Stimulation
Simultaneously squeeze my nipples
Finger my pudenda
Devour my clit
Pandora's Box begins to shake
Flick your tongue on my hardness
Introduce your mouth to my labyrinth
You have found the key to Pandora's Box
Put your finger in my mouth
Let me suck on it
Concentrate on the warmth
The softness of my tongue
The feel of my lips
Imagine
The combustible ending
When I put my lips on your pillar
Now turn the key to Pandora's Box
Release what I have held within
Pandora's Box is OPEN

§

This whole experience has my
thoughts all over the place. He has ex-
pressed deep feelings to me already.
Not sure what I am going to do. I can
say this, my ego won't allow him to
just fuck me up all crazy and not re-
turn the favor. I have been severely
lusting for him. My desire to take him
into my mouth has now become a need.
These nasty, freaky thoughts trump any-
thing else right now. Besides, I know
better than to make any decisions when
your mind is filled with deviant, sex-
ual thoughts.

I stood up in front of him. My eyes told him exactly the mood I was in. Smirk on my face, licking my lips, eyes giving away the hunger I have for him, I told him in my sultry voice "it's my turn to play." Also, "compliance is a necessary factor, do not disappoint. What a perfect spot indeed my love. What is about to take place, it needs to be hidden even from the angels."

I took out my phone, because the song I wanted was specific. It was Janet Jackson's Anytime, Anyplace. Can you hear the sultry beat? As the song began to play, I began to wind my body in tune with pulsating beat. I never broke my gaze from those beautiful brown eyes, neither did he. Oh, there he goes again, sizing me up, ready to pounce and devour. No love, that was not in the instructions I have yet to give.

I got closer to him, parted his legs. I then turned my back to him to give him a lap dance that included my wicked wind and belly dancing skills, combined. I threw my head back and rested it against his body. As my body swayed to the sultry beat, I softly sang the lyrics as if they were my own. With his grip tight on my thighs, his dick began thumping in the middle of my ass. The pressure and friction caused me to drip into my thong.

As I sang to him, he begged me to take my thong off so he could put it in his mouth and suck on the crotch. I seductively turned around, looked over my shoulder at him and said "no baby, I must deprive you just for a while." You have already had your meal. I know you desire a second feeding, but not right now. Now take your hands off my hips, and don't speak unless I require your voice. He thought to himself, because he dared not speak AW SHIT! I would have never expected this from her, what an amazing woman! How do I know? His facial expression told me.

I stood then turned around. I brought him back to me so I could taste my own sweetness mixed with his flava. I was now ready to return the favor but he was trying to resist the idea. I allowed him to speak, he said he enjoyed and savored every moment, enjoyed bringing me unspeakable pleasure, holding me while I quivered under his tongue, allowing myself to be vulnerable to him was his pleasure indeed. I sang the part of the song to him in my sultry, seductive voice "I don't give a damn what you say (I changed the words a little) I want you now!

SN: now I know what you are thinking. All this resistance, he must not be clean. Lay your worries aside. I secretly had his medical records pulled before we met.

I let him know, that is what your mouth says. However, the throbbing dick in your pants tends to disagree. I told him he needed, even desired to be tended to as well, my pleasure. However, since you don't want me to put you in my mouth, I will show you how skilled I am with my hands, you will not be disappointed, I promise.

I lubricated my hands with my own wetness so they would slide easily up and down his dick. Switching places now, I laid him down. As we were changing positions, the song Slow Dance by Keri Hilson played softly through my phone. I sang to him "something happens when we slow dance" and "your body's calling me." All sense gone, all senses electrified. Perfect.

I used my pointer finger and thumb to hold my vice grip at the base while I squeezed and stroked his dick with pure pressure. I stroked him down, and then back up. When I go to the tip, I squeezed hard, opening my hand just slightly as I worked a circular motion at the tip only. My other hand was working the base and his balls. Moaning, lightly fucking my hands. Mmm yes. It did my ego good to see I still have some skills up my sleeve. We are not nearly done yet.

I then straddled him, having him sit up just enough so he could reach my lips, all the while still working his dick to the point of explosion! He was solid, thumping, growling, and calling out to me like he needed saving. I told him to suck on my titties, which he hungrily feasted on. He loved my voluptuous breasts, sucked on them as if they would give up milk. Shit, I was enjoying it just as much as he was! Oh how erratic he was becoming. I have to slow this down.

Ah Ah, not yet lover. I took my tit out of his mouth so I could have his mouth. We kissed each other with wild untamed passion. I sucked his tongue and bottom lip until he could barely breathe. I got off him so I could lay him back down, and seen he had a little precum escape him. So I licked the tip of his dick while I was still stroking him, and then kissed the tip with my voluptuous lips. He couldn't help but continuously sit up and wonder who this woman is! The pleasure I was giving was enhanced 100 fold!

He followed my rhythm and moaned, growled in pleasurable pain. Just the state I wanted him in. I took both of his balls into my hand and stroked his magnificent pillar with my other. Since he said no to what I wanted, he had to suffer. I put just the tip into my mouth, and sucked the tip of his head only while I worked him. He was in no position to resist, so I took advantage of. I put both of his balls into my mouth, used my tongue to massage the man's equivalent of a G spot. Now, he is fucking any part of me he can! He is over the edge. YES!

I could feel the surge in his veins, I could feel his dick was locked and loaded, ready to shoot off his

seeds. Now his growls are primal, rav-
enous letting me know my suspicions are
correct. He is about to cum. That is
not what I'm aiming for. He needs to
have an orgasm too. I want that body
twitching! I will not settle for less
than that. One good orgasm deserves an-
other, right? I thought about slowing
down, even stopping so I could let him
cool down and bring him back to the
brink of ecstasy. I decided against it,
he had suffered enough. I wasn't trying
to sleep in the park! He was vulnerable
now, looking at me with pity and rage.
He looks like he wants to be released
and break my pelvis at the same time!

So I took his dick into my mouth,
swallowed that beast whole! Straight
back past my tonsils then hummed on
that mutha fucka, WORD. I sucked hard
and fast, using my tongue to work cir-
cles around his dick while I was suck-
ing!

After some hard sucking, I used my
hands to stroke him, with lightning
speed and precision, altering between
squeezing him hard and softly. He
grabbed hold of the bench and was
thrusting hard with a pace that was
hard and steady. As he did, I kept tak-
ing it straight to the back of my warm
throat, still humming the entire time
so he could feel the vibration.

Finally, he let out a growl that
would've called the whole pride home if
we were in the jungle! Eyes rolled to
the back of his dome, toes cracking

from being curled so tightly, and then exploded in my mouth! I drank his seed like it was a hot southern day and he was a refreshing glass of lemonade. He struggled to sit up as he nervously tried to catch his breath. He actually checked his surrounding because he forgot where he was for a moment!

My lover locked eyes with me, engaging me in this staring showdown. Of course, I had a devilish smirk on my face. TOUCHE love is all he could muster up to say, with an exhausted giggle. He said; "if this is what you can do with your hands and mouth, WTF would you do to me in the bedroom?!" Who knows, I responded with a chuckle. We kissed each other with sweet satisfaction, our flavors combined together in what was the most delicious, most delectable combination I ever tasted. Shockingly, he has a very good diet; fruits are definitely a staple, for the both of us.

We didn't care if anyone saw or watched us. We were not arrested or approached. I'm sure there was an audience who enjoyed the show! It was just us under the watchful stars twinkling above us. We walked back the same way we came. I was thanking GOD he lived very close. Our hands were interlocked with slight rocking, gazing into each other's eyes as much as we could. Our smiles bright enough to guide our way back on the path.

However, his gaze held something different, more than a twinkle. It was as if he was looking straight into my soul, wanting to intertwine with my spirit. He told me he never felt this way before about anyone, how much joy I have brought him from our first conversation. How I am able to hold him from his core. His intense gaze began to make sense.

Is he contemplating making this official? How am I going to keep my husband from finding out about this? Right now, he believes I am away on a cruise with my best friend! That lie was easy, because I said we were going to a place I have been before, so it would be easy to describe what I seen. And my BFF? She got me!

Just as I was taking my phone out of my pocket to turn it off…

Adanna, who is that man on your screen calling? Why does it say "MY LOVE?"

FUCK. MY. LIFE.

§

A Partner after the Creator's Heart

I am sitting by the pond
The wind envelops me with warmth
It blows through the trees
They begin to hum their song
HE IS MY N, S E AND W
The sun sits high in the sky
Caressing me with its penetrating rays
They travel deep within my spirit
Burning out all worries
Without burning me
Surrounding me with natural love
Warming my soul
HE IS MY SUNSHINE
The sky is a powder blue
So clear it seems as if you see heaven
There is nothing hidden that it won't
willingly reveal
HE IS MY CLEAR BLUE SKY
The grass is soft under my feet
Massaging them with every step
The swans are at peace with the warm
waters
Floating along
Bobbing with the harmless waves beneath
them
The waves provide a special softness
under them
This cannot be explained, only experi-
enced
The birds are singing their beautiful
song to whoever will listen
I THINK OF MY LOVE
How he sings his sing song to me
With every word spoken
So filled with love

His love coils around my spirit
My soul
My essence
We are one
I am sheltered from all things
That would harm my heart and mind
HE IS MY PROTECTOR
My strength my joy
He is never to be a part of pain
HE IS MY COVERING
His touch ignites me
Every nerve yearning for more
I am so sensitive to him
Sending a vibration through me
Like no other can do
I only respond to him
HE IS MY LOVER
He invites me into him
He knows I am his shield
Guarding his heart and mind
He knows I bring no pain
Suffering
No anguish
HE IS MY UNIVERSE
Only the love especially created in me
Before I was born into this earth
Is for him
I am his surrounding warmth
His shelter lies with me
He supports me in everything
I encourage him
Making the path beneath my feet soft
He is the grass beneath me
He removes all out of my path
I won't experience unnecessary pain

HE IS MY COMFORTER
He holds me
He feels good to me
Only his body beneath mine
Gives me unexplainable feelings
Special between him and me
HE IS THE GENTLE WAVE
His thoughts are clear to me
Nothing hidden within
HE IS MY CLEAR BLUE SKY
His breath in my ear is warm
Intoxicating
I get lost within his thoughts
HE IS THE WIND THAT BLOWS
THE BIRDS THAT SING
THE TREES THAT SPEAK A SING SONG WHEN
THE LEAVES MOVE
The great Creator of all things
Provides his love to us every day
In the natural beauty around us
Go outside
Put your head back
Close your eyes and be silent
Listen
Can you hear HIM, feel HIM?
DIVINE LOVE is in everything around you
It is like putting your head on The
Creator's heart
HE loves you
HE is not just in the storm as many
songs state
HE IS THE MOONLIGHT
THE STARS TWINKLING
THE RAIN POURING DOWN
THE SNOWFLAKES THAT FALL
HE IS IN THE BEATING RHYTHM OF YOUR
HEART

So when he sends you your mate
You will be able to put your head on
his chest
Listen to his heart
And find the song within
Only you will understand
A MELODY WRITTEN JUST FOR YOU
In a language the outside world
Will not understand
THE CREATOR IS LOVE
And HE will be sure
All these qualities are within
The partner that is for you
Someone after his own heart
LISTEN FOR HIM/HER
This person might not be perfect
Your family might reject him
But you will know
Because of the hidden song within
REMEMBER
A PARTNER AFTER THE CREATORS OWN HEART
Someone especially for you
If he/she has not come yet
Don't fret
They are being prepared for you
And you are also
Being prepared for them
WITH LOVE

S

Revoke the Contract

This is a FICTIONAL story you are about to read, but it happens in real life. I wanted to talk to you for a second. There are many who are at their wits end, and choosing to give up instead of fighting. I know what it is to keep a smile on your face, when you are going through it! Not wanting to burden people with your problems, because they have problems of their own. So many are in pain, but to anyone who is reading this, know that you are not alone! I know the thoughts can be overpowering, and stress can get out of control, but I ask that you PLEASE talk about it! Trauma is the tree, and the roots run deep. You have no reason to feel embarrassed about what you may feel. Your feelings are valid, and they are real. If you can't or don't want to talk to anyone you know, there are resources out there where you can call anonymously and lay your burdens down, without judgement! You matter, you are beautiful, and you are the stuff stars are made of, literally! ***THE NUMBER LISTED BELOW DOESN'T MEAN YOU WANT TO HARM YOURSELF!*** You may just need to talk, and maybe get some help for your situation. I want everyone to feel radiant and beautiful, inside and out no matter what the skin color is, your size or your crooked smile!

Every Person Matters! Don't let anyone or anything take your shine! **NATIONAL SUICIDE PREVENTION HOTLINE 1-800-273-8255**

§

She was tired of dealing with the hand life had dealt her. She wanted to end it all, but she couldn't do it by her own hand. Too selfish and egotistical to do such a thing. After all, she was very concerned about what people would say about her, even after her demise. So, she waited for Death itself to present to her, and she would go quietly into the night. Feeling so low, she thought Heaven didn't want her and Hell didn't deem her worthy, and the present plane she was on only tormented her day and night with gleeful joy! There was no peace, anywhere. Until she found *PEACE,* in herself.

Yes Mr. Stockbridge?
Please come into my office in 15min.
Certainly.
My heart started racing, palms sweating, and my mind processed a thousand thoughts a second. What did I do? Is it because I was 10 min late the other day? Did Sherline tell that I was on a private call? What could he possibly want? I know I have been doing a good job! What the Hell is it?!

I stood up from my chair, put the screensaver on, adjusted my clothing and walked towards the office. Once I got to the door, I paused for a moment to take a deep breath to calm my nerves. After this quick ritual and prayer, I knocked on the door. After being granted permission to enter, I opened the door…

Good morning Ms. Bailey, take a seat.

OMG, this can't be good! Not Makeba today?

Greetings Mr. Stockbridge, how are you?

Fine. Look, I appreciate you leaving your previous job and coming to work for our company.

Maybe this IS a good thing!

You have been an exemplary employee.

YES.

However,

OH. SHIT.

There were unforeseen circumstances that has come about, and I am sorry to tell you, we have to let you go.

EXCUSE ME?!

Yes, this is effective immediately. You will not be able to finish the work day. As a formality, security will be at your desk in 15min to escort you to HR to do your exit interview. Once again, I am sorry and I wish you the best of luck.

Just like that? Why? I left my job for this company!

As I have already explained Ms. Bailey, unforeseen circumstances. Now if you will excuse me, I must make a call.

I stood up, completely speechless. Then, I got pissed and knocked his shit right off his desk! I stormed out of the office, not without slamming the door so hard the glass broke on the door! Sherline tried to ask me what happened, and I told her to mind her fuckin business you dirty BITCH! I never liked her anyway.

Security was already at my desk by the time I got back. Not surprising, but I simply didn't care. I told them it would be in their best interest to just let me get my things and not touch me, at all. The tone in my voice and the scowl on my face told them I meant business. Without a word, they stepped aside and let me complete my task. After I gathered my things, I was escorted off the property. No need for that exit interview I guess.

I put my things in the trunk, slammed it and got in my car. After sitting for a minute, I screamed and beat on my steering wheel with tears running down my face. "I am so sick and tired of fuckin losing"! I shouted over and over again. It was at that moment a thought crossed my mind, but that's what I let it do, just keep going. After my episode, I sat there, chest heaving trying to catch my breath. Then I turned the key, threw my car in drive and drove to the nearest bar to drown my sorrows. And that's exactly what I did.

After the bartender cut me off, I left and went home. (it must have been by the grace of that being they call GOD because I was TWISTED) I threw my keys on the table, dropped my purse to the floor and sat on my sofa, sulking. The tears began again, but it wasn't just for the day's events but for all the times I tried and blessings just eluded me. The past played out in my mind like it was fresh, and not 5yrs ago. This frustrated me even more. I could not control the flashbacks, and it was driving me mad! Then another thought crossed my mind. But this time, it slowed down a little as I tried to force it's exit...

I decided to take a shower and wash off all of the day's events, along with the thoughts of the past. Not sure if that was the best choice at that particular time because I was so intoxicated. Why? Because I didn't realize I had fallen out of the shower! but of course that would happen, life has conspired to torment me. And so it continues!

I have to admit; I was a bit on the grouchy side. Well, let me tell the truth, I was a straight up ASSHOLE who had an expectation for everyone around me to just deal with it, because of my situation. Well, that was unfortunate for me to have that belief!

There was an unexpected knock on my door. When I opened the door, it was Robert, my man. I have to admit this as well; I was not in the mood! I sucked my teeth and stepped aside so he could come in. He didn't say a word, and kept his head down. Wait, he has never done this before. Naw!

Look Makeba, I didn't want to do this over the phone, because I feel you deserve better than that.

WHAT? You're cheating? I KNEW IT!

No, I am not cheating, you have to be in a relationship to do that.

What do you mean? You ARE in one!

No, I am not. And if you weren't ignoring my calls and acting like a complete and total BI-, no I won't call you that. You have been unreasonable and cold-hearted. I have done nothing wrong to you. Yet, you treated me like I was the enemy.

I AM SORRY BUT YOU KNOW WHAT I AM GOING THROUGH!

I do, and I am sorry. However, I am unhappy and not willing to allow you to drag me down into your abyss. I am done.

FUCK YOU ROB! GET OUT OF MY HOUSE!

Gladly. Best to ya, Keb.

§

BITTER

I've been pierced through the heart
Out of my mouth I released blood
But it isn't really that
I spit out rose petals
Imaginary heart shapes
Because although Love is gone
It existed at one point
I wasn't always this cold
Life
That's the way it wants me to be
Your touch
soft
Like a rose petal
Hearts
A symbol of Love once before
I must regurgitate this feeling
Purge you from your place of existence
Evicted
No longer reserved for you
LOVE
It feels like an infirmity to me
Something that will rot me from within
I have to accept the loss

But who says gracefully?
A nasty one I am now
BITTERNESS
Welcome

§

Rob walks out, and doesn't even
slam the door! How DARE he not fight
for me! He never loved me anyway! I AM
SO TIRED OF LOSING! "You see, you will

never win, everything you touch turns to dust." The thought now seemed to be a voice, and that's what it said! I spun around to see who was there, but it was no one. it scared the SHIT out of me! but, I was drinking though so I was just buggin. That rage inside continued to rise, and I was not sure I wanted to stop it. Tired of feeling pain.

Cheryl!

Hey Keba what's the matter?

GIRL! I have had the crappiest of days! First, I was laid-off from that new position at that job I told you about, THEN THAT NO-GOOD ASSHOLE decided to break-up WITH ME! now what am I supposed to do? I don't have nearly enough saved to keep me afloat! FUCK MY LIFE!

I am so sorry to hear that! OMG, I don't know what to say…

I was SO pissed off, I slammed that door so hard it shattered the glass and I knocked everything off that arrogant jerk's desk!

Lol! That certainly sounds like you, but I don't think that was the best way of handling it. Did you apply for unemployment?

Yeah, but could you believe him?!

Well…

WELL WHAT??

You see, that. You have to learn to control your temper, and not take it out on those closest to you.

REALLY??

YES. And I have to go, I am at work now. I lo-

I hung up, more pissed than I was! Let me make myself a drink to calm my nerves. DAMN IT! I tried my best to be ok, to shake it off, but I couldn't.

One day, I walked by my full length mirror and stopped. I back tracked and took a look. The thoughts began immediately. Maybe I am not sup-posed to be happy, to love or even to smile. Damn, look at my body, my weight is like a yo-yo and all these stretch marks are all over the place. UGH! Look at my face, just full of acne! I cri-tiqued every inch of me. looking back, that's when darkness began to settle in. I began to loathe myself, and blame everyone for that feeling. The signs for low self-esteem, which has SO MANY accompanying roots.

1. Social withdrawal
2. Anxiety and emotional turmoil
3. Lack of social skills and self-confidence accompanied by depres-sion and/or bouts of sadness
4. Less social conformity
5. Eating disorders
6. Inability to accept compliments
7. An inability to see yourself 'squarely', meaning to be fair to yourself
8. Accentuating the negative
9. Exaggerated concern over what you imagine other people think
10.   Self-neglect

11.   Treating yourself badly but
   no other people
12.   Reluctance to trust your own
   opinion or anything enjoyable
13.   Expecting little out of life
   or yourself
Yep. That's me. except I gave that
heat to everyone I thought would even
think about pissing me off…yep.

§

   I had to run to the store, because
I was almost out of everything. I
didn't like leaving the house. I just
didn't have the energy. I didn't talk
on the phone, answer my door or do any-
thing that would cause me to leave my
bed. I was in deep in depression.
   While I was out, I noticed a man
with both legs amputated. This normally
would not cause me to bat an eye until
I seen a runner go by. I watched the
legless man watch the runner. The look
on his face told it all. He would give
anything to have his legs back and be
able to run. Then I looked at mine, and
felt a pang of sadness and appreciation
at the same time. I didn't speak to the
man, because well…I just didn't want
to. I went into the store, got what I
needed and went home, quickly.
   When I got in, I immediately took
my clothing back off, all of it. When I
went back to my mirror, that voice be-
gan to speak. "you need to lose weight,
you are ugly and fat and no one wants

you!" as I began to entertain the negativity, it seemed a stronger voice spoke, but more gentle. "You are still here, you have all of your limbs and you are beautiful!" I thought of that man and the runner, and decided to silence that negativity! Although I am not a mother (yet) I read this with pride. And so should you!

§

MY BODY IS PERFECT

The flower that blooms during adversity
is the rarest of them all ~ Mulan
My body is perfect
Because it is mine
Nothing sucked
No fillers added
Until you have had to fight for your
breath
You cannot appreciate the beauty that
is me
It is perfect to the man who is perfect
for me
So many get caught in the outer beauty
To find it is a sess pool within
What is it exactly you are swimming in
Ask yourself
So many wind up marrying a frame
Which holds nastiness
My belly bares the marks of life
The veins in my legs
Reveals the weight I carried
My breasts less perky

Because they contained the food that
sustained the life I brought forth
The bags under my eyes reveal the tire-
less efforts
To provide
Care for
Nurture
Sustain
The life I brought forth
My smile
Original
My own
Teeth not perfectly lined
Still declared beautiful
By EVERYONE I have met
The man for me will say
I admire you my Queen
Cherish you
Respect you
For you
In all your perfection
When he is inside me
He digs for the living waters within
Panting
Sweating
Grinding
Stroking
Does not mind the work
Do you know the vessels in the womb
Resemble the tree of life
He does
He yearns to be one with her
Every time the river overflows her
banks
He comes alive
She has fed her love
She is satisfied

Oh how she loves to feed him
He loves his belly full
This water is sweet
Quenching
He knows what he has
Embraces her curves
Rests comfortably on her soft body
He smiles
No filth here
No artificial preservatives
All natural
Pure love
To many
I am not beauty
Too fat
Out of shape
Maybe
Perfection is in the imperfection
Why do you share your opinion with me
I have no interest in you
There is nothing original about you
Your depth perception
Is that of a child
I never asked for your thoughts
Yet you share them with me
What about me has caught your attention
What has sparked the flame within
You need a conversation with me
Cling on to my response
I laugh
You anger
I see who you are
Perfectly
You have no idea who I am
Nor will I reveal this to you
I don't toss my pearls to pigs
Will not drop my handkerchief

In front of a rabid animal
Does it shock you I don't have low
self-esteem
Or shock you that you do
Why else would you come for me
I didn't send for you
Run along imp
These are deep waters
You belong in the shallow end
My body is perfect
FOR ME

§

I'm sorry I have been behind on my rent. But I left a job for what I thought was a better position, then they laid me off 2 weeks later!

Judge, although her story is a sad one, my client is not running a free shelter. He has expenses and a family that has to be taken care of. So, although we sympathize with Ms. Bailey current situation, my client has been patient enough.

But your honor, I have lived there for 2 years, never late on rent before!

This is a true statement, but it has been 5 months without any monies received, not even a partial payment. My client cannot go on any further with Ms. Bailey. We are asking for an eviction order.

But I have nowhere to go!
Ms. Bailey, you have appeared before me several months ago, I held off granting

the eviction to give you more time. Your landlord had no complaints about you. As a matter of fact, you were an ideal tenant. However, I must agree with the plaintiff in this situation. Although the court sympathizes with your situation, I am granting the eviction order.

I sobbed heavily...I couldn't speak.

Your honor, we thank the court for hearing this case and granting the order. We ask also that all back monies be paid through a levy of wages when Ms. Bailey begins employment again.

WHAT?! How am I supposed to get on my feet? Joseph, you know you don't need the money! Joseph!

DO NOT ADDRESS THE PLAINTIFF!

Sorry Judge Montero.

Ms. Bailey, you cannot expect to live for free. I must agree, because you still occupy the residence, the plaintiff cannot generate any income, and must also spend more money to restore the unit for the future resident. The request will be granted.

ARE YOU SERIOUS?!

Yes, however, I will give you 3 months before the levy will go into effect. The gavel slams, and the decision is final.

I walk out of the court, only to find a tow truck outside, in front of my vehicle! Aw SHIT!

I run up to the driver and ask; "WHAT THE HELL IS GOING ON BECAUSE I STILL HAVE TIME ON THE METER?!" That fat FUCK (I know, my mouth is filthy) said; "ma'am, I am here to repossess this vehicle. There have not been any payments made in the last 3 months, and no contact with the dealership. I have matched the VIN number with the paperwork. I am sorry, but I have to take it. May I have the keys?"

I said "NOOO! Please don't take it! Just tell them you couldn't find it yet!" He responded; "I am sorry, but there is GPS on your vehicle, and mine. I will not risk my job so you can keep your vehicle. Keys please?" "FUCK IT! TAKE THE BITCH!" I said as I threw the keys at him.

I called Rhonda this time, and when she answered I didn't give her the chance to say hello! I just began to spew out what had happened as I clutched my purse and walked up the street towards the bus stop. I was unable to hold back the tears. After cursing the very ground I walked on, I got even more infuriated and hung up on her too. I never gave her the chance to say anything! She called right back, but I didn't answer. What else was there to say?

Once I reached the stop, I sat down on the bench and contemplated my next move. Then I remembered, I applied for unemployment a few weeks ago, and I was sure I would get it. I decided to take a breath, get to the house and begin to pack it up, along with making some phone calls to be able to rest my head somewhere.

I swear it's always one thing after another.

Once I got home, I quickly went to check the mailbox, and lo and behold, there was an envelope from unemployment. I breathed a sigh of relief, and went to my apartment. For some odd reason, I wanted to wait until I got inside to open the letter. After I got inside and opened it, I understood why instinct told me to wait. I guess so I wouldn't act a fool in public again...

Dear Ms. Baily,
I regret to inform you your application for unemployment has been denied, because you are mean and violent BITCH that couldn't restrain herself from acting like a rabid animal in the workplace. There is absolutely NO WAY we will give you anything! Furthermore, don't bother to file for an appeal, because we will deny that too! This decision, along with everything bad in your life is nobody's fault but your own! Now you have a good day, NOT!

Well, that's not exactly how the letter was written, but that was my interpretation. Just when I began to come up out of a low place, there life came and put its foot on my neck, and kick me back into that hole. Fuck. My. Life.

After throwing a silver-back gorilla tantrum, I had to find someplace to stay until I got on my feet. I began to make some calls...

Cheryl? Hey girl, how are you?

Good hun, what's up with you?

I need to ask you a favor.

What?

I need a place to stay for a little while. The eviction was granted. My car is repossessed and unemployment denied me.

WOW…damn, that's a lot girl, but I can't help you with that, my husband's mom is here with us, and there is no room. And, we just helped one of his friends out of a bind, so our money is tight. Sorry girl!

I understand, sorry I asked. I will figure it out somehow. Well, I have more calls to make so I will talk to you later.

I never bothered to call anyone else. I just knew it would be the same story. And, I just wasn't ready or willing to hear the excuses. Feeling beyond drained, I grabbed a bottle and went to bed. The negative thoughts raced in my mind. But this time, they weren't going *through*. This time, there was no exit. Those thoughts *lingered!* I was dancing with darkness…

I had a bottle of hydrocodone's I was given after some dental work. I steadily heard "go ahead and do it, it could all be over and no more pain." I took a big swig of the alcohol straight from the bottle. As I reached for the bottle, something bubbled up from deep with me! It was warm, kind and soothing! It was as if everything in me told me not to do it! I heard a proverb that basically said; "the beast that wins is the one you feed." It was at that moment, I decided to kill the one with the sharpest teeth!

I started to call on people I knew, but decided against it. Somehow I knew, it would only aggravate me further, and that was unacceptable. I knew I didn't need a conversation, but an ear. But who? Who could be a neutral party? As I was contemplating this, and trying to silence the negative energy, I turned on the TV, and the commercial came on, as if on cue. I listened…I dialed the number, and it was one of the best decisions I made in a long time!

REVOKE THE CONTRACT

The demon speaks into the ear of the
confused
It will try to make you turn on your-
self
REMEMBER
They can never feel the warmth within
the heart
They have been forever separated from
love and compassion
They detest those who have the capabil-
ity to *FEEL*
It whispers nasty things
The unclean one will make you believe
the false is true

Now you're standing on the edge of des-
pair
It won't physically push you
HOWEVER
It will taunt
Leave you no room to breathe
It lies to you
Telling you in order to experience
calmness
Let go of the rope!
Take that step!
You will never have true happiness
Darkness is all you will know
Joy is elusive
Give up on trying you will never win!
No one is there for you
No one loves you
This voice gets so loud
You can't hear the screams of your
loved ones, begging you to step back
into their loving arms!
You can't see they have always fought
for you
Because the scales on your eyes distort
your perception
Your body begins to shiver as if going
into shock
This is the body's reaction to preserve
your heart
It pulls all the blood to the vital or-
gans
Even it doesn't want to die
The demon is frustrated
It taunts the things around you
Distraction, Confusion, Despair, Hope-
lessness, Emptiness!
It's what it must make you must feel in

order for its victory
So it will not suffer for its failure
There is a light on the horizon
Small but seen, it's calling to you
Speaks gentle whispers
Encouragement, Peace, Joy, Happiness
and Love
It's in abundance, it surrounds you
It's in the form of life
Family, Friends, Strangers yet to be
friends, Flowers, Oceans, Birds sing-
ing, Sunrays, Warm embraces, Laughter
The struggles must happen, beloved
In order for a star to be born, there
must be a collapse
An explosion, for new life to come
forth
This is not your death, not destruction
But a new birth, YOU!
The star is born!
In order for a flower to come to be,
the seed must die
The shell must be broken in order for
life to spring forward
You have mistaken this separation as
rejection
Yes, it opens the door to loneliness
and a feeling of abandonment
But you must see beyond the dark
Still those negative voices
You are in the process of ascension
You are loved
This journey may be a solo one
You can't remain in the same place
It's time for you to become your des-
tiny
Childish things must pass away

Fulfillment is at hand
The things you dreamed about
It's time!
Step back from the ledge and hold on to
the rope!
The universe will pull you up, it will
embrace you
Fall back it will catch you!
In it is the Creator, Infinite Love and
Beauty
The air you breathe
REVOKE THE CONTRACT you secretly made
There is no life in darkness!
Come, Embrace love and LIVE!
I tell you, beautiful BELOVED
It is just a season, this too shall
pass
REVOKE THE CONTRACT

§

On the other end of that phone, I found
invisible friends! I was able to talk
it all out, confess things I could
never tell anyone I knew and found my
path to peace! Now, that doesn't mean
things didn't continue to happen. I
wound up in a shelter, and lost my
things because I couldn't afford the
storage fees. But, I found that talking
it out helped me to clear my mind, let
go of the inner rage and think clearly.
I am back on my feet, got a better (and
stable) job and my own place. Oh yeah,
and BOUGHT my car! Things last for a
season, indeed. Sometimes, the season
is long. I learned to weather the

storms and get through it! And yes, I apologized for my behavior to everyone I hurt (except Mr. Rosenberg and Sherline) LOL!!

§

Patiently I Waited

What is it you want
Rather who are you waiting for
One should not wait for the perfect
person
There is no such thing
Maybe you are so closed off
No one can approach you
Angry black woman
Still suffering from past hurts
I just want you to open your mind
Not wanting a relationship with you
I am seeing someone
Just trying to help you out
You have serious issues
So beautiful you are
Yet so cold within
Judgmental you are
Game player
You think you understand
The male psyche
If you did
You wouldn't be alone
Are you there
The silence is deafening
I am here
It is polite to allow you to speak
Are you finished
You accused me
Let me testify
In my secret closet I spoke to the uni-
verse
Consulted with The Creator
I want a BEAUTIFUL man
I am willing to wait patiently
God answered me

He actually gave me his name
He has loved you longer than you know
I have been preparing him for you
He will be your husband
Do not treat him like a fantasy
He is real
I spend time with him
Discreetly
No need to announce it to the world
We are establishing ourselves
Every word said is a seed that is
planted
What a perfect garden of love we have
Just the two of us cultivating
Out foundation is laid perfect
Because there is no intrusion
Opinions, I heard he
I saw him, He used to
Tainted words
They seep into you
Like pesticides
Supposedly they help
Still poison
Our bricks are laid to our perfection
The house we build on top
Will not crumble
From outside sources
This investment solid
Only the Creator may deposit
HIS return is our vested love
We make no early withdrawals
To invest elsewhere
SELAH (think about it)
Now to you
Who gave you permission to educate me
Who asked you about your thoughts on my
situation

You have shown me your foolery
Intimidated by wisdom
Trying to show me your guts
Left them spilling out of your abdomen
You are the perfect example
of the man I do not want
No desire to get to know you deeply
What purpose would that serve
Your dialect sounds like that of wisdom
to the untrained ear
HOWEVER
Your words are laced with immaturity
I never listen to what you say
It's what you're not saying that
intrigues me
Thank you for keeping my skills sharp
That is the reason we talk
You said you were trying to educate me
I am still waiting
I understand the male psyche perfectly
This is why no one has ever left me
All stay close
The wise know me
No part of me is ever hidden
However
I also understand
The cloak the universe has around me
You have not had the privilege
To see the great beyond
Things like
Your favorite color
Musical preferences
Enjoyable past times
Are of no use to me
Save that for the one
Who desires an EROS relationship with
you?

AGAPE is even too much to ask
My dude, we are cool
You have mistakenly placed me
In the box of typical women
I am far from this grouping
So as for me
I patiently waited
And she has granted me the perfect man
For me
I stand corrected he says
You are truly a Boss Chick
Excuse my reference
I smile, you are excused
And are a good listener now
Further intrigued you are
Lay at the feet of your elder hun
I have much to teach
Your numeric age means nothing
When you are speaking to a Sage
I need to spend some time with him
Just him and I
He and I hid in The Creator's shadow
We rested in the Almighty
I allowed God to prepare me
Bathe me in precious oils and fra-
grances
Meditated on what my ancestors in-
stilled in me
Before I became a form in this world
Preparations are complete
The destined time has arrived
I must excuse myself
He has waited long enough
PATIENTLY

§

I've Touched my Dream

My love Kamau, your name means quiet warrior. Certainly, your name fits this description. I have known you to not only fight, but win in anything you put your mind to. This is also true in matters of the heart, especially mine. What we shared, it was so intimate. Our spirit and souls intertwined as one. We became a strand unbreakable. Until now…The evening cruel fate caused a supernova-like explosion in our worlds, separating us from a life of blissful love. What remains is silence, fragments of what we once shared continue to float in the wind.

My name is Akinyi, meaning born in the morning. My parents said I was the sunshine in a very dark time in their lives. Whenever life tried to cast a shadow over their life, once glance at me would make the clouds part, blue sky's visible, and the warmth of the rays brought happiness, joy, and peace. However, there were times in my life when I couldn't find that inner light for my own use.

What the hell? Can anything else go wrong? Am I a walking omen to myself? Why does the universe conspire against me? Diabetes is getting the best of me. My dad died suddenly, just leaving the rest of us to pick up the pieces and go on. A part of me is envious he escaped this cruel world. My job is now trying to conspire to terminate me, my ex has become a stalker, and the management of my building is trying to get me out! Now I have to quit school on top of all of this, how am I supposed to sort and deal with all of this?

After going to see my primary care doctor, he determined I can no longer perform my job duties. I was on the verge of a complete meltdown. He wrote my letter of resignation, along with a slew of medications and a trip to see a psychiatrist. "Going to see someone" has always been frowned upon in my community. It was considered something Black people just don't do. Well, this was going to be an exception because I have to save the little bit of me I had left.

It felt good to release all of the hurt, pain and sorrow I was feeling. I cried many tears, broke a vase and cursed the ground that my enemies walked on. Thank God she understood. My previous person was a bit afraid of me. It was determined that I was no danger to myself, just to all those around me. Maybe it was because during one of our sessions, I kept glancing at the vase on the table with a sinister look (according to him.) Dr. Mallory asked how I was feeling this day. I answered honestly "I'm feeling a little edgy," while now staring at the vase. The session lasted no more than 15 minutes. More medication added to my daily diet.

Lacking any interest in outdoor activities, I turned to my computer. Several of my friends were raving about several social media sites; supposedly I can meet people from all over the world from the comfort of my home. Food had become my friend; it soothed, satisfied and filled me with its love through delicious flavors that would just explode in my mouth. 40lbs later, I realized it was now a harmful relationship I needed to get out of. Meeting people from the comfort of my home? It's time to give it a try.

I chose one site in particular; mainly it was because of all the invites I received before I signed up. I said to myself thank you girl! After creating a profile and uploading my pictures, the response was incredible! I could not keep up with all of the photo comments and requests to be added to my friends list. At a time in my life when I didn't love myself, it felt good to chat with people who could see the beauty in me I couldn't see myself.

There was one person in particular who caught my eye. His name is Kamau, I loved the name, and it sounded exotic. I spoke his name in my sultry voice, confirming my thought. Handsome, light skinned, green eyes, 6'2, medium build and lips that made you wonder how they would feel pressed against my hot box. Damn! His body language indicated to me he was the sensual type. You can tell a lot about a person through a picture, if you want to see what's there. I may not know a person personally; however, I could recognize a person's energy. It felt right. I was now determined to make him mine. Akinyi's fire has been ignited!

I was not one to request anyone, but I secretly prayed he would request me. He did, YES LAWD! Shortly after I added him, we exchanged numbers. It was one of the best decisions of my life! We would talk for hours about any and everything from the stars in the sky to last night's dinner and never run out of things to say. He was quite the gentleman, nice. However, I was ready for more; ready for that other side of him I know is there. I was ready for him to make me leak, pulsate…it's time to play!

He could sense I was ready to take the conversation to another level. Maybe it was the hints I was throwing at him; "do you like my body?' Do you love my lips, breasts?" Kamau was a good listener; he also loved to indulge me. Anything to put a smile on my face was his pleasure. So attentive he is, I was about to find out just how attentive and giving he could be. He will also learn today that I am not the delicate flower he has determined I am…

I was surprised by a delivery this particular morning. I checked to sender information, it was from Kamau. I thought it was something he purchased for me, but I was wrong. When I opened the package, it had a white tank top and a note. The t-shirt was his, with his scent all over it. I brought it to my face and inhaled deeply. Damn this man smells so good! The note simply stated I was to be wearing it when he called promptly at 9pm. Also set up the tripod with the camcorder, the monitor with speakers, and drape your bedding with the set I provided. The phone was not to ring more than once. If it did, there will be no activity tonight. I love a take charge man! Compliance, done!

In anticipation of this love session we were about to embark on, I made sure I spoke to all the pertinent people I needed to, showered, and lit several scented candles. The mango, strawberry, peach and blackberry scents blended together in the air, created a tropical paradise in my home. To add to my personal paradise, I also turned on the cascading waterfall on my mantle and opened the window to let in the rain-kissed air. I adorned the bed with the most exquisite bed linen, red satin sheet set with a black panther in the middle of it. I was simply blown away. I was anxiously anticipating my call when the phone rang…

Akinyi, turn on the camcorder, return to the bed, and sit up slightly with the pillows propped behind you. I want to see your face, never close your eyes, and never divert your gaze. Yes, baby. Place the phone on speaker, and

let's play. Before we start, let me ex-
plain why there are no props. I will
connect directly to your energy, what
was placed deep within you for this
specific moment. This encounter will be
like no other; I will touch your ero-
genous zone, awaken living waters and
entwine with your spirit self.

I want you to part your legs, let
the cool air caress your alter of love.
Imagine my fingers immersed in the
place that gets hot and moist, unable
to dry its self out despite the intense
heat building within. I have caught
your scent, electrified are my senses!
Chakra gates open now, correct? Imagine
your fingers as mine; put your fingers
in that pussy!

While my fingers explore the vast-
ness of your subterranean pleasure
spot, I feel the soft ridges of your
walls, your pussy muscles squeezing my
fingers, begging them to go deeper. The
tightness, the heat, the pulsating
rhythm has aroused me. I introduce my-
self to your g spot, so she knows that
I am the last person she will ever
meet, desire, and yearn for. I hear her
talking; she speaks to me through the
gasping of your voice, gently moaning
to catch your breath. Soon, she will
scream obscenities…

Kamau, my She is engorged with
deep passion and longing to feel the
heat from your mouth, the pressure from
your tongue, you know my rhythm...your
fingers explore the pink pleasure,

stroking in and out of me, I take them in my mouth to delight in the essence of me. While you're there, I want you to taste the sweetness that lies within. Feast on the meal I have presented before you. Did you come with an appetite? Insatiable SHE is, Pink Panther. SHE will not tolerate your failure to please, this is the land of milk and honey...

She is my Deity, I will worship her, bow my face into her palace, lunge my tongue in and quench my thirst with her succulent waters! After quenching my thirst, tasting the honey that flows before the milk, I stop to nibble and suck upon your luscious clit as she calls out to me to take her deeper inside my mouth to stroke, taunt and tease.

My Eze, you take the air out me, I am breathless! It's so hard to keep my focus on the camcorder when you are igniting me like this! You are engulfing my clit, slurping, lapping, finger fuckin annihilating the pussy oh shit! I move my thighs from your shoulders; I need to brace myself against the waves of ecstasy! Arching my back I grab the sheets, I am not in control! Winding my hips as thrust into you, OH FUCK it feels so good! Dripping my nectar, you won't waste a drop! Heat intense, throbbing uncontrollable, energy surging, chakra gates open! I need your lips, your tongue against mine, let me taste ME...

My love, I comply with haste! The greedy tone of your voice, the lustful glare of your eyes compels me to meet your tongue with mine! You grab my face, I kiss you deeply, twirling, rolling thrusting my tongue inside your mouth! You begin sucking, biting and licking your elixir off my bottom lip! Shit girl! I nibble on your neck, put pressure on that other spot that sends tremors straight to the puddy!

Grabbing my head, pushing my face back to your nether regions, wrapping your legs around my waist as you brace for another eruption! MUTHA FUCKA I'M ABOUT TO CUM! My body is no longer within my control! My breathing is erratic, eyes fluttering, heart pounding, back arched, fuckin the air, toes curled AH DAMN! Eyes have rolled to the back of my head, pussy throbbing, fingers drenched, body convulsing! I let out a deep breath, try to steady breathing and heart. Now, let me take you there.

As I compose myself, I look at the monitor to see he is stroking himself at a steady, almost slow rhythm. I hear him faintly moaning, I see he is trying to maintain control, I will fix that. My love, I sit up and give you a mischievous glance. It's my turn, and I plan on making you experience pleasure beyond what your mind can comprehend, you ready? This will go well for you.

I let go and put you on your back. I sit on top of you; my pussy is saturated with that sticky. I sit on top of your dick. Don't you dare try to nestle inside of her until I say so. I love the delectable flavor of you and me, so I passionately kiss you. I leave your lips, and then my tongue slithers down the middle of your chest, and kiss you until I reach your nipple. I flick the tip of my tongue, take it into my mouth and suck, gently graze my teeth back and forth over it, I make it hard and wet then blow. I'm squeezing, twisting the other, simultaneous pleasure.

Keep those hands up, you're not allowed to grab your dick! You writhe; revel in the gratification I am delivering. I move on to where I yearn to rest my mouth…he's thumping, waiting to feel the warmth of my mouth now. I slither my tongue further down, my ass in the air, rocking side to side. Baby, I'm hungry! He's been waiting for me...

Akinyi, you're fuckin with my emotions right now, put your dick in that mouth! Let me see what it can do! I'm grabbing your head to put this beast into your deep cavern…I am in control; take your hands off me! I run my hair over your dick softly, and then I take the tip into my mouth. You slightly jerk at the sheer pleasure I instantly brought you. I love the way you feel inside my mouth.

I wrap my lips around your pulsating rock hard dick. My tongue embraces you as it is swirling and slithering. I trace your bulging veins, and then I blow softly. My hands are stroking you, continuing to trace the veins with my tongue out of my mouth so you can watch. I seductively watch you enjoy the show, thinking to myself "he has no idea I'm going to devour him."

Your balls are in my hand, gently massaging them until it is their turn to be warmed with my awaiting mouth. I suck you from the base to your tip; deep throat you only once because it's not yet time to devour. I get back to the tip, where I softly place the tip of my tongue inside your dick to taste your pre-ejaculate. He beckons me to kiss him, so I oblige, muah! I then put your head back into my mouth; I have to feel it again. You continue to drip and throb; I continue to stroke and suck! I can feel the tingle that travels from your balls to your opening before you explode but AH AH AH, not yet.

YOU PRETTY BITCH! Got me screaming obscenities and shit! Fuck! I'm going to split you in half! Fuck you until I break your fuckin pelvis! Shit! I kiss you on the inside of your thighs in search of your erogenous zones. I find one and there and suck on just the right spot, that feels good huh? I go back to your dick, and take you straight to the back of mouth, DEEPTHROAT! I hum so you could feel the vibration as I siphon you like I want to pull all of your seed out of you, massaging you with my tongue, squeezing your dick so tight my cheeks are drawn in, as I draw out your will to resist my control over your dick, then back to the head I go...

OH BABY he moans, grunting, panting and growling I can tell he is about to lose control! The pace has quickened, vulgarity spewing, and his voice has deepened. However, I can't have that. I have not granted him permission to finish. A bossy one I am, and am proud of it! He tries to speak, I tell him to be silent, and I am still speaking.

As you thrust yourself in and out of my mouth, I alternate the pace, the pressure. I suck you softly then hard, pausing to marvel at what is before me, to let my tongue do what it does, I take you into my hands and stroke you, there is an area unattended to, I take your balls in my mouth and massage them with my tongue as I am stroking you, you're pulling my hair, thrusting into me, moaning from the depths within. I find your g-spot, I know your rhythm, my hands are stroking you with lightning speed, you throb in my hands, pre-cum dripping from your dick, I go back to taste you, MMMMM, so good...

I AM ABOUT TO CUM! You're causing me to experience this pleasurable pain and I hate to love this shit! As I watch him on the monitor, I could see he was not joking! Now his toes are curled, and he is fuckin the shit out of that fake ass he has pulled from somewhere! His grip so tight on that ass I am sure it would leave bruises if that were me! He is screaming at me, AW SHIT! FUCK! YOU FEEL SO GOOD! CAN I CUM ON THAT PRETTY FACE?!

NO you may not! Take your dick out of that ass, and beat him until I see that nut go projectile! Come on baby, give it to me! I want your whole body involved! Bust a big one for me! DRENCH ME IN ALL YOUR WHITE GOLD! Make me rich baby! I want to hear you grunt, growl, let me see that scowl on your face. GIVE THAT SHIT TO ME NOW!

With that, his body convulsed, his growl primal from the pit of his gut, and that ejaculation shot straight to the ceiling! It was the most intense finish I had ever seen a man experience! So beautiful that was. He said "DAMN," It was all he could muster at this time. Hell, I came again just watching him! No shame at all, I loved every minute.

Akinyi, I have to tell you that I love you. I have never felt such intensity for any woman in my life. Please do not think it's because of this. The dance we will soon experience physically is secondary to what we have experienced. You are my friend, and I have much admiration for you. I simply adore you. Do not be surprised if I present you with a ring.

Silently, with tears in my eyes, I stared at the monitor as he kept his gaze on me. I was speechless! Never had I imagined he felt so strongly about me. I responded; "I love you too My King. You are the man I have been waiting for, the man my soul yearned for, and yet patiently waited for. If you present a ring to me, know that I will accept my love." We said goodnight, I love you to each other, and turned off the equipment.

He became the reason I soundly slept at night, and looked forward to the sunrise in the morning. No need for all of those pills, he was all the balance I needed in my life. He inspired me, supported me, and encouraged me at every turn no matter what the situation. I could not wait to see him. Has the universe stopped its relentless assault on my life and allowed love to enter my life? After speaking on the phone for months, he decided it was time for us to meet.

Akinyi my love, I am sorry I have to leave you for some time. I have no control over this. Please know, I would never walk away from you. You have been my blessing from Divine Love, and I will cherish you, always! Our conversations, our connection was on a plain beyond the stars. Our spiritual connection has the feel of a past life between us, familiar spirits on an endless journey to find one another each reset of our life on earth. I love you, beloved.

Infinite Love

She taught me how to smile
She taught me to feel without fear
To trust
To love
She was not born just to die
She was put here on this earth for
me
I do not accept my departure from
her
My lifeline, my heartbeat, my rea-
son to LIVE
I was at war within
My mind, My soul
My spirit, My heart
They each fought for control
The mind
The devil's playground
Because it is unable to love
It literally has no sensation of
any sort
The heart
Where Divine Love resides
Because it feels, it beats
It reacts protectively to the
slightest violation in energy
Your brain can die, the heart will
live
Your heart dies, everything fol-
lows
She was able to bring them into
alignment
A harmonious agreement
She helped me starve the darkness
and feed the light

The beast in me only released when
my Love is threatened
I will be her covering, she will
be my shield
I will cut through the very fabric
of time and space to be with her
I tell Heaven NO because she needs
to be in my arms
But if it ever came to this
I would die so she can breathe
Call out to me Beloved
Your voice will guide me back...

§

Alas, the meeting would never take
place. A week before we were to rendez-
vous, I had a dream about him. He kept
apologizing for leaving me. I couldn't
understand because I knew he wasn't
dead. That same day, I couldn't reach
him, which was highly unusual. Later
that day, I found out a drunk driver
hit his car as he traveled from work.
He immediately slipped into a coma, in
which he remains. I have no idea where
he resides; his family will not dis-
close the information to me, or anyone
else.
Kamau, it's been years since you
left me physically but spiritually you
have stay connected to me and I have
always left my heart open to you so
that you can reach me. However, your
family has kept you from me for reasons
unknown, despite the fact they know who
I am to you. I held on as long as I

can, refusing to love another. You feel like a fantasy that will never be. I love you past the deep recesses of my heart, my soul and spirit intertwined.

I know it is the same for you, because when you got into that accident you came to me in my subconscious and apologized for leaving me. At least your family plays the voice recordings, and shows you the pictures I send. I am told when you hear my voice, even in that limbo that you live in you would smile, drop a tear.

We have a love so deep no devil in hell can interfere. However, with a heavy heart I have to let you go. I have tried to maneuver in this world holding on to you. It is not healthy for me. I feel enmity towards your family which is beginning to consume me. This does not mean I don't love you, or will ever stop praying for your recovery. I keep you before the Creator, on the altar.

I must believe if we are true soul mates, the universe will correct this and join us once again. Once you awaken, our love for each other should create an invisible path only we can see. My scent in should be carried to you, a scent only you will recognize. This will ignite lost memories, you should be able to close your eyes and feel me. Remember me my love, you must find me again. I guess the universe had not been finished with its punishment…

Heartbroken

I'm lying here looking out the window
The sky seems to be black
Only a few twinkles in the darkness
I wonder, does the universe know what
lies within my heart?
Is it empathetic to the sadness within?
Is it aware that I am in pain?
He said he loves me, I believed him
So why did he leave?
Why didn't he fight the beyond?
Why did he go quietly into the night?
I know I'm being selfish
This is the part of love unspoken
I want him here with me
The sky is like a mirror of what I feel
Seemingly empty, Only a few rays of
light
The light seen is the love I have for
him, as if the light itself fights to
remain seen
Light that will not retreat into the
depths of a void until unseen
My heart won't settle down
It won't stop calling for him
I wonder can he feel me
Does he know I'm close?
Alas
I have some pictures
Archives of past conversations
Is this all I have
Is this the only way to keep him close?
How can he be kept from me?
Why did the universe create that bridge
to keep us apart?
How can he function without his heart?

Keaka

Working in a credit counseling call center, I listen to the same stories every day. Parents and college bound kids looking for money to enter a school they cannot afford. However, the calls never stay on course. My voice, I am told is like silk brushing across the skin, sexy, even exotic. I am of Hawaiian and African American descent, and my accent is unusual and rare. Somehow I was able to infuse my parent's accents into one, mesmerizing anyone who would listen to my voice. After a physically, verbally and emotionally abusive encounter with insanity personified, (which also ended my career) my self-esteem was at an all-time low, until the call that awakened the Mistress in me, and I became the Queen of the Perverse. This is the title given me by my faithful slaves. This will have to be told in 2 parts…

My name is Keaka (pronounced key-AH-kah) which means person of shadows. (as you read my story, you will understand how my name fits.) I am a single woman living in NYC. My place of residence lies within the heart of the city that never sleeps, and where big dreams come true. Fashion is everything in this robust city full of diversity and undiscovered dreams. However, I had fallen into a lifeless, unassuming routine. I rise at the same time daily; up and out at the same time, clothing

barely thrown together, grab my book
bag, hop on my bike, Starbucks stop and
arrives at work. I blend in to the
background, never noticed or recog-
nized.

This was not the life I had envi-
sioned for myself! I, Keaka was a suc-
cessful hotel manager of The Erogenous.
The most secluded, private and prestig-
ious hotel secretly located the heart
of NYC. You could not use any internet-
based search to locate this venue. Ex-
clusive and salacious, this is the
venue where the fallen angels play.
There is no demand that could not be
met. The darkest and evil of fetishes,
fantasies, and propensities are
granted.

However, you absolutely MUST meet
all requirements before entry is al-
lowed. All references, medical records
and assets are thoroughly checked. If
there is a problem, then it becomes a
problem for all parties involved; the
one that referred as well as the one
wishing to enter. Honesty is the best
policy; anything else will be hazardous
to said person's health. The gatekeep-
ers employed possess the emptiness of
the deepest abyss.

My exotic beauty; long black hair,
caramel skin, dark cat-like eyes, high
cheekbones, full lips, hourglass figure
with hips that hypnotize as I saunter
along the street made me the perfect
choice for what this hotel caters to. I
am the epitome of beauty in society

standards. The ability to cater to the wealthiest clients every whim discreetly made me an all-time favorite, always on demand. However, there is a limit to how much I could handle. To keep my sanity, I had to break away from the sometimes sadistic clientele. When I am finally free, I love to explore the vibrant night life of the city that never sleeps.

My position allowed me to meet many powerful and influential individuals. I was able to utilize the privilege to have VIP access to the most exclusive night spots in the city. There was no need to ask questions, because this was now an expected occurrence. Our heels are never less than 5 inches, our attire, hair, and makeup always flawless. When we walked past the long line straight to the bouncer, our walk was that of royalty. The snickers and sneers was a welcome sound. It symbolized we were on point.

The DJ was on fire this night! The heavy bass from an apparently immaculate system vibrated my chest, the crowd was hyped, and barely any space on the dance floor. There were many empty seats; bartenders busy, an indication this night was going to be an amazing time! The girls and I danced our way to our VIP table. Anxious to get our cocktails going so we can dance until we feel our feet again!

This was one of my rare nights out with my girlfriends, and I loved every minute of it! I have seen several of my clients enjoying themselves, however I couldn't help but wonder if they would require my services at the evening's end. I shook the thought because tonight was mine; they would need to deal with my very capable assistant manager. One of my girlfriends nudged me and threatened to kick my ass if I continued to think about work. She knew me well.

As we were enjoying our complimentary bottles (courtesy of Steven, he LOVES his puppy play parties) several suitors approached the table. One guy in particular had on enough cologne to be able to actually taste it! He had a gold tooth, rings on almost every finger, and clothing from 3 generations passed down! Shoes leaning so badly I put money on those ankles giving out and his knees snapping soon! I am convinced he is not a natural bow-legged man. With a bottle in his hand, he began his greetings with DAMN MAMA'S! Y'all sho is fuckin beautiful! I wanted no parts of this one.

I began to scout the room, when I happened to look towards the bar. I made eye contact with the most handsome man I had seen in a long time. Smooth chocolate skin, hair and face cut to precision perfection (oh did she have a weakness for this type of man) almond shaped eyes, a strong chiseled jaw line with the fullest of lips (good god I can feel them on my pussy right now)!

Standing at least 6'2 with an athletic build, I am sure if I was to stand now, I would leave a wet spot on my seat and this milk would drip down to my knees! LAWD talk about that sticky! I mistakenly used the term "this type of man," When I should have said "this GOD!" So, my weakness for a man built in the image of a GOD is absolute!

He began his short journey to our table. He had a walk so confident it seems as if people simply parted as he walked through the crowd. The music appeared to have grown silent; the people seemed to have disappeared. Time itself felt like it slowed down. I could not look away, blinking was not an option.

Put into a trance, I seen my future with him with every step he took. Once he reached the table, my girls stopped all laughter, eyes fixed, mouths practically hanging open as they prayed to the gods he was coming for one of them. Their prayers never went past the ceiling, because he was there for me!

Let me say, I was never one to believe that I would ever take an interest in any man I met in a club, at least not anymore. For me, there was only one agenda on everyone's mind and that's who is fuckin tonight! How do I know this? Because I was one of the authors on the book! LOL!! It was my sole mission when I stepped out in my younger and more reckless years, to get my back blown out! Hell, every girl in my squad was like-minded! We all have a past, right?

However, I think too highly of myself to fall into that foolishness, even after Henny shots! But now, my system has been put on overload! Shiiit! I am ready to bag this magnificent GOD TONIGHT! This is straight BS, because listen to me! He done brought out HOEISHA! I laid her down A LONG time ago! What does this evening have in store for me?

The Approach

I felt you before you made an entrance
A thought I kept to myself
No one else in the room could hold my attention
Because I was so consumed with this incredible feeling
My heartbeat felt like palpitations
When you entered the club
Your eyes
Those hips
Your lips
Those VOLUPTUOUS breasts
DAMN
Everything changed
The air
I could taste you
Your essence
DELICIOUS
Now fate
I see what you have in store for me tonight
Its been so long since we danced

Your patience will be rewarded my love
Fate responded
I trust you my darling
I acknowledged
So it is, so shall it be
I wondered
Did she feel me too?
Now I know why I had to stay
Planted in place at the bar
The universe must have been privy to my
conversation with fate
Satisfied that resolve had been made
This union
It will excite the GODS
Our first touch
EVENT HORIZON
There will be no escape from the gravi-
tational pull
EXQUISITE
POLISHED
I am sure
CHARMING
She has my seed shooter on leak
Her pudenda will drip on site
It's time
I have so much in store for you…

§

Good evening ladies (damn that
smile) he greeted the table occupants.
(That is how I see them right now!)
Then he turned his attention to me, and
with a deep baritone voice he said
"good evening Miss" (damn right I'm
single) as he extended his hand to re-
ceive mine. I lightly laid my hand in

his palm and responded with a playful "greetings" and a smile. His hand was large, masculine and strong, yet gently held mine. An indication to me he is able to control his body. His thumb, long and wide, middle finger to the wrist damn there long as a pencil! This is an indicator of what his dick will be like (that's right ladies; the feet have nothing to do with it). LAWD I have to calm Ms. Vaginista down immediately!

He held his stare, it would seem I am not the only one that had experienced the trance. He apologized for the lingering hold of my hand and the intense (my word) gaze without introducing himself. I laughed lightly, making sure he was able to see my beautiful smile in action. He said "my name is Michael, and you are?" I said "my name is Keaka." I seductively raised my eyebrow as I stated my name. He was enchanted and intrigued, exactly what I wanted. At that point, I decided I was DETERMINED to hold his attention for the rest of the evening, maybe longer than that...

Michael then asked me to join him on the dance floor. In my mind I'm screaming HELL YES I WILL! But that would not be lady like. I'm sure he noticed the slight trance he had me in. I couldn't let him see me in like that again. I've slipped but have not fallen. Never letting go of my hand, I rose from the table and joined him. I practically forgot I was not there alone. I would have stepped on their pretty faces to come out of that booth to be with him! My girls were yelling something, but I could have cared less what they were saying. Maybe I should have...

It was as if I were gliding to the dance floor. I do not recall my feet touching the floor. I was being led into the future, my future with Michael, and it looked magnificent from my view. Once we were on the dance floor in the spot he was comfortable with, he turned and pulled my body close to his. He placed his hands on my hips; I put my arms around his massive shoulders, and we gyrated to the thumbing beat. That was not the only thing thumping…

As we danced, we would briefly separate to show our moves, sometimes doing silly things to make each other laugh. I loved his smile; it seemed to illuminate the room of darkness. Indeed, it were as if we were the only ones on the dance floor, the as if the DJ played only for us. It was simply magical, and incredibly delightful. This was an evening to change the rest of my evenings. I welcomed it.

Keaka, I must step away for a moment. Please do not leave this spot. I want to easily return to you without having to search. I promise I will be right back. He took my hand and kissed it. I blushed, then nodded my head and briefly closed my eyes when I did. Yes, I will stay, go ahead. Thank you Queen, I appreciate that. He kissed me and again and disappeared into the crowd. Inside I was screaming THANK YOU THANK YOU! I wasn't quite sure who I was thanking, but whoever in the universe would accept it, I gave all honor to that gracious spirit!

I glanced at the table, only to find it empty. I am sure the bottles were as well. They were somewhere on the dance floor, probably violating their dance partners body. As I laughed to myself, he returned. He took both of hands, leaned into me to reach my ear and said "just wait." Keaka, I love to say your name. It is exotic, like you. You certainly are a stunning woman. Would you allow me this dance? And with a wink and a smile with a wink and a smile the tempo changed and Keri Hilson's song Slow Dance began to play.

He gently pulled me towards him, placing his arms around my waist and giving me a playful squeeze. One hand found its way to the small of my back, the other to the nape of my neck. I wrapped my arms around him and rested them his shoulders muscular shoulders. Starting from the back of his head I softly let my hand glide down to the nape of his neck several times, up and down. Then, I let my hands rest again with one wrist upon the other. At this point, a song of my own began to take place in my imagination.

Slow Dance

Hey baby
Listen to the sound of my voice
What is it I want with you
I want to take this instrumental ride
with you
Make me beg for mercy I do not wish for
you to grant
Taste everything that is me
Touch Lick Suck Explore Thrust Throb
The heaving of our chests
The depths of our breaths synchronized
The sweating of our bodies
The stickiness of our juices mixing
with one another
Will bring us close to the stars
Our private heaven created as we climax
We will appear as falling stars' humans
wish upon
Tonight
We make love like the Gods in spirit
Take this instrumental ride with me
Let's make magic
With this slow dance…

§

    We began to sway in sync. I loved
the way Michael controlled my spine,
massaging my neck and gazing deeply
into my eyes. I laid my head on his
chest as we began to rock. Swaying our
bodies side to side, keeping our love
zones grinding on one another. It was
as if our bodies took over without
thought. I fit right into him. Pressed

so closely to my body, I was intoxicated by his pheromones infused with the scent of his cologne. The room seemed to fall silent although the music was loud and the voices were many. Flashbacks of a past time when our souls once danced together under a bright moonlight came to mind. Yes, something is happening with this slow dance.

This song is truthful Keaka, something is happening as we slow dance. I am intoxicated by your scent. Your skin is soft, hair like silk. I am not saying this just to get between your legs; I am sincerely recognizing the beauty that is you. Please know, I did not just notice you when our eyes finally locked. I saw you at your entrance. I watched your graceful stride as you boogie bounced your way to your table, lol. I went to the DJ because I needed to know how you felt in a sensual way, not just with you throwing your ass on me. You feel just as I had imagined you would Queen.

I lifted my head from his chest. Looking up at him I was almost entranced again. After quickly shaking that off, I shook my head. I was stunned; however, I had to laugh at the humor he injected into such sultry statements. I lightly hit him on the chest and just continued to smile. We never looked away to any other part of the room. Did I say I love to look up into a man's eyes? It is one of the best things in the world to me.

The way he was burrowing through me, it was like he was trying to find a sign of our past life. I have to admit; I was doing the same thing. This was an enchanted encounter, and I loved being lost within our slow dance of a life's past. We were making love with our souls in that spot. Embracing what we both were feeling; intense passion, yearning, longing for the touch lost in our momentarily parting in the past, this was everything.

When he finally broke our gaze to look around, I did so at the same time. We were so engrossed in each other; we didn't notice we had a small crowd, which included my girls giving me the look of "girl we HAVE to talk!" we also didn't know the song ended, the beat changed and we were WAY off! We let go and laughed so hard and blushed at the same time. I was secretly hoping for more evenings like this. We fell in line and continued to dance a little bit more, throwing my ass back on him. Funny thing is he did the same!

I looked back at the table, and the ladies had regrouped. I thought it would be rude to never go back over and talk to them, although that's exactly what I wanted to do. Once the song ended, I politely excused myself to go talk with them. He understood, kissed my hand and asked me if I was good, was there anything he could get me. I said

I was fine, and then he told me he would be at the bar. We stood still for a moment. I can't have time freeze again on me! Shook that off once again and playfully asked why he was still standing here.

I want to watch you walk away, marvel at that magnificent frame, and be sure you get back to your table ok. Is that alright baby? I am not going to walk you over because I'm sure the ladies are probably mad I kept you from them so long. We laughed, but he had no idea how right he probably is! If you all need a refresher, let me know and I will take care of it. I kissed two of my fingers and placed them on his lips, smiled and walked away.

FATE

You have yet to disappoint me
She will do just fine
Her confidence
The arrogance
I detest that in her
She walks as if she is the only
one in the room with beauty
Her PRIDE
I will destroy it
Behaving as if she knew I was going to come for her
Retched maggot
I am sure her friends are going to
warn her about me
BUT
She is already in too deep

All I had to do was stroke her EGO
She won't listen
That is a good thing for me
A good predator always catches its
prey
I will enjoy every minute of this
Do return soon
My weak little fawn...

§

As I walked to the table, I couldn't help but think about how right it felt. All my senses were ignited at once! Then I immediately tried to convince myself it was too good to be true. However, the thought would not take root in my mind. Have I found love in the club? Is he the one I have secretly asked for in my heart? Have I found my husband?

After I got to the table, my girls were in a FRENZY! They were all speaking at the same time, with panic in their voice. I tried to ask what the fuck was going on, but I couldn't get a word in edgewise. I slammed my hands on the table to get them to shut the hell up! Once I finally got their attention, I asked again, what is going on?

GIRL! You HAVE to leave that man ALONE! Some woman came to us and said he is an abuser! He is very controlling and possessive! Do not be fooled by his smooth approach, this is not the first time he had met someone in THIS club and made their life a living HELL!

BITCH! You betta run the other way as fast as possible! FUCK! I didn't bring my knife tonight of all fuckin nights!! I will GUT THAT BASTARD if he tries ANYTHING! FUCK IT, I will use these stilettos and plunge them into his temples!

WHAT?!

Keaka, I don't think that girl was lying. I could see the look of sheer terror in her eyes! As a matter of fact, she left immediately after telling us this because he is here. I think you should take heed to what she is saying.

I don't think so! She is probably a bitter ex who does not want to see him with anyone else! I just had an AMAZING experience with this man, which I might add I have not had in a VERY long time! I will not let you heffas ruin this for me!

KEAKA!

NO! I will not hear of any more of this bullshit! Now if you will excuse me, I am going back to the dance floor with MICHAEL! I LOVE YOU GUYS but PLEASE let me have this evening?!

I walked away from my loving friends, well more like sisters with a pain in my heart. I knew they only want what's best for me. Looking out for my best interest at heart. I have to admit, right now I am not interested in any of what they are saying. I am not thinking with my head right now because I am more interested in GETTING some head! Man, my shit is screaming obscenities at me right now! Every step I take is like stimulating Pink Panther! There is a perverse fascination welling up inside of me. This could very well be the wrong move, but I am not in control right now! I have to find him!

His energy is intoxicating, refreshing and exhilarating! There is something within me he has awakened, and I refuse to walk away from it! But, could me girls be right? Am I trying to dance with the Devil under the strobe light?

As I was walking back to Michael, I noticed a side grin on his face. I thought to myself; "yes girl, he is going to devour me tonight!" But I later realized, I was wrong…

There you are beautiful.

Yes, here I am.

Let's go to a quieter and intimate spot. I would love to talk more, without shouting to the top of our lungs. It kind of makes my ear sting when you have to speak into it so close.

I thought you would never ask! (I did not tell my girls I was leaving, didn't feel like arguing) I didn't think I drank a lot tonight, but I feel very intoxicated. Maybe it's because I have not had any alcohol in a while and it's just hitting me a bit harder than normal…

We left in his vehicle, my girl had a spare key, so she would be able to take my car. We arrived at his place, which was absolutely gorgeous! He lived in a high-rise, where privacy is of the upmost importance. In my profession, I understand this completely. The doorman gave a head nod and a smile as we walked in. the staff greeted him as if he were royalty. I was very impressed, which dropped my guard. Privacy? Expensive high-rise? That head nod and smile? Looking back...

"Keaka, have a seat. Let me slip those shoes off your feet for you. Your feet MUST be killing you," he said with a playful chuckle. I did so without a thought, because he was SO right! After he did that, he went into the kitchen and came back with 2 *BACCARAT DÉGUSTATION ROMANÉE CONTI GLASSES* priced at $475 per glass and a bottle of *CHATEAU LAFITE* 1787. That wine is almost $157,000 a bottle! (yes I am shouting with a fancy tone lol.) This man really knew how to make a girl feel like the Queen of England! I should not have been so shocked though, his furniture was obviously imported, because this leather sofa I was sitting on was definitely a contemporary piece, and the material was butter-soft! The rugs, the art, the chrome...everything just exquisite. I am speechless!

We talked about, whatever because I can barely remember the conversation. I wasn't focused on his words, and I think he knew that, because of more than one reason. But apparently, my words weren't really spoken in a clear manner. I was slurring my speech. How do I know? I will tell you in a minute. But, let me get to this part.

He guided me to his bedroom, which held a king-sized bed that sat up on a multi-level platform. After laying me on the bed, he meticulously began to undress me. I gave no resistance, this is what I wanted since we danced at the club, that much I remember. It was as if he was worshipping every part of me.

"Keaka, you are so unspeakably beautiful, radiant and delectable. I absolutely must explore every inch of you." Lifting my dress, he pulled my thong down ever so slowly, all the while kissing and licking just on the outside of Pink Panther (wink.) his full lips made the hairs on my body stand on end, my temperature began to rise, and I was pulsating. I impatiently sat up to remove my dress, sloppily and uncoordinated. Who cares right? As long as it came off! After sliding my laced barrier down my legs, he let his locs fall onto my feet, and then slid them up my legs until he got to my knees. He then used that thick, moist tongue to slither up my inner thigh. I grabbed his hair and wrapped my hands in it to force him into my honey pot! Defiantly, he wouldn't have it…

"FUCK MICHAEL!" I slurred and shouted in pure blissful ecstasy! I was gone. He stopped right at the opening to the place where the roots to the

Garden of Eden began. He inhaled deeply, and let his breath out steadily and controlled. The way it hit my sticky made my whole body jerk! Parting my thighs wider, he lightly touched the hood of my clit with his tongue. I was pulsating so hard you could see it! Devious bastard!

Suddenly, he devoured my pussy in one gulp! He had his whole mouth covering me, and his hurricane tongue did not miss one crease, crevice or hidden spot! I mean FUCK! I never felt a tongue pulsate like that! Smacking, slurping and me gasping and screaming is all that went on! This man was HUNGRY and I had more than enough to feed him! Of course, my pearl extended out from under the protective hood, and he feverishly sucked her until shockwaves were sent surging through my body! I swear I had an out-of-body experience!

He roughly pulled me down to the edge of the bed, and threw my legs in the air parted as far as he could get them and thrusted his dick inside me WITHOUT MERCY! I tell you he right back to my cervix! He went so far back my past life encounters flashed through my mind! He pounded while grinding, burrowing himself into me without a thought about how painful it was to me! He had a look on his face…contorted, almost non-human. The sounds that emanated from his throat to his mouth was…alarming. He had total control of my body.

Once I began to try to stop this session that was more like an assault, he completely lost it! He began to punch me all over my body, yelling things like "YOU SMUG BITCH, FUCK YOU!" the vulgarity and hate that literally spewed from him was blood curling! He seemed to have wanted to focus on my face. I did my best to cover it with my arms, to no avail. Shortly after, I passed out. How did I know all that went on? He recorded all of it! Apparently, he enjoyed watching the brutal assault.

I woke up in a hospital bed a few days later, with my girls around the bed. Their swollen eyes let me know how grave the situation was even before I demanded a mirror. They were concerned when they realized I left my purse at the club, and there was no way to find me. They began to call around to the hospitals until they found me. I love them with everything I have in me! We all sat in silence, outside of my muffled cries. I didn't feel like I had the right to cry loudly, because I didn't listen. But my girls let me know there was nothing to be ashamed of, they were there for me, and not one "I told you so" left their lips. Michael had money, and it spoke louder than any witness would.

I told my boss what happened, but not the condition of my face. I thought that after some time, I would return to normal, but that didn't happen. There was a scar that could not be completely covered with make-up. In my job, there had to be absolute perfection. No exceptions. However, I thought because I was so loved and did a superb job every time that maybe there would be one. no chance. I was told "you cannot be the face our clients see, because of your imperfection. We are sorry this happened to you, but this is a business. Your services are no longer required." And, "do not forget the clause, it would be regrettable if you do. Consider this your favor. Goodbye."

That was the beginning of my dreary call center life. On this particular day, I received a phone call that changed my life…here is an introduction to the new path that laid before me. I will tell you more in the next installment…

§

Three Way Touch

Good evening love
Have you prepared yourself
Is your resolve made
Extraordinary and memorable
Mischievous
Obstreperous
This is ME
I vow to you this night
This encounter
This engagement
Will have three of your future genera-
tions
Born quivering
Auscultate
Concentrate
OBEY
Robust moaning
Substantial groaning
Vigorous growling
Required
If I am displeased
I will punish you
With silence
My voice
Silky
Soft
Alluring
Now FOCUS
My unsullied one
Take your position
Lie on your back
Mirrored ceiling sufficient
Watch yourself

As you listen intently to the sound of
my voice
Allow your legs part
Grant yourself the pleasure
Stick your fingers in that pussy
Lick your juices
Spread your legs
Massage that pearl
Coax her out
Squeeze your tit
Do not close your eyes
Watch yourself
Remember
OBEDIENCE
No hesitation tolerated
I'm with you baby
NOW
Let me hear you moan deeply
Arch your back
Writhe
That pussy
Nice and wet now
Unsettling to you I know
Yet
You cannot resist
But you must
For a moment
I know
You ache to feel my warm mouth on your
body
Don't you?
Good
Now rise
Do you see the briefcase in the corner?
Go to it
Password MIND FUCK
Open it

Look at you
Fascination
Trepidation
Titillation
Pick up the items
Hold them in your hands
Become familiar with them
Explore the shape with your hands
This moment I grant
Because from here
You will be thrust into a world unknown
to you
Erotic pleasures
Delicious indulgences
Your chest is heaving
But your breathing is controlled
Good girl
Swallow hard
You can still taste yourself
Take a long breath in
Now deeply exhale
You will learn today
Why the whisper of my name among the
elite?
It provokes throbbing in the Love zone
The Rabbit
The dildo
You will use all simultaneously
Take your position
Put the dildo on the floor
Suction it
Custom made
Vibrates
Circular motion
Looks small huh
It will expand with every stroke
There is a surprise with this device

Anal penetration
Now
Get the rabbit
Place it over the X on the floor
You will need to hold this for a moment
This one is modified
Now SIT
The rabbit in your pussy
The dildo in the ass
ON
Let go of the Rabbit
It doesn't need your assistance
Lifting from the floor
It begins to stroke you deeply
The prong-like appendage
Grips your clit
Massaging your engorged pearl
Grip your tit
Lick your nipple
Pull your hair
BOUNCE
You will not finish unless I command it
OH OH AHHH OH
I hear you
I can no longer use a soft term of en-
dearment
My obedient one
We have begun our exploration
You filthy BITCH
That shock That sting
The burn of the opening of your ass
Pleasurable pain
The awakening of your hidden senses at
once
YOU'RE WELCOME
I will be back...
Now back to you light foot

I have not forgotten you
I see you have enjoyed the show
Obedient you are
Didn't make a sound
You shall be rewarded
You are moving into place as I speak
Perfect
The same rules apply
DAMN
(I lick my lips because I am ignited)
Submissive creature
I will appease your secret fetish
I am your MASTER
Now lie on your back
I see your dick is hard
Lubricate your hands with what I pro-
vided
This is no ordinary lube
I know what you want
You will be pained
Stroke that dick for her
Feast on her screams and moans
Sounds of pleasure
Obey me you fuckin maggot
Cunt
Make sounds of dick sucking
Smacking Popping Kissing
You better be still fuckin
Back to you my submissive creature
Pinch your nipple hard
Bite your lip
Draw a little blood
Let me hear you breathe
Grunt and growl
See it in your mind
Fuck her pussy
Fast Hard Brutally

Let your imagination rule you unre-
stricted
Your tongue is deep into my pussy
Suck slurp FEAST
Let your growl produce a snarl
Bring it from the abyss of your throat
Be the savage I command
Your MASTER desires it
NOW
Get the fuck up
Do you see the briefcase?
Go to it
Password MIND PENETRATION
Open, take the paddle
The leather neck restraint
The rope
The dildo
The pussy and ass
Put the restraint on your neck
Loop the rope as instructed
Fasten your dick to the pole
Your pussy and ass too
Both custom designed
She will tantalize the tip
Get on your hands and knees
Now fuck that thing deep
Throw that ass back hard on your dick
You should feel the effects of your
lube
Teeth gliding along your dick
Lean forward
Choke yourself
Pull your hair hard
Pleasurable pain
NOW STOP
You are not allowed to cum yet
Get up

Release your restraint
See the door?
Go into the other room
There she is
She is your DOMINANT
Now girl
Get the shoe string
Tie it around his balls
Loop around his dick
Tighten
LIGHT FOOT
Lay on the table
Do whatever she commands
I leave this to the imagination
Make him scream
TRUST
He will LOVE it
ENOUGH
It is time
PENETRATION
So many openings
So many toys
Walk over to the nightstand
Open it
So many delights
I am confident
I have ignited your imagination
You have invited in the dark side of
the moon
Explore
ENOUGH
NOW
FUCK FUCK FUCK MY BITCHES
FASTER PRIMAL
YES
SCREAM PAIN
INDULGE IN PLEASURE

GROWL GROAN SHRIEK
RELEASE
My Pets
You may call me The Queen of the Per-
verse
For all of you looking in
My name is Keaka – person of shadows
You will not find me in person
Exclusivity
That is my code
Until next time
Think of your darkest fantasy
I will be there to fulfill it…

§

Love
and
Revenge

US

My love
Before I became a we
A you and I
An US
I couldn't wait to fall asleep
I knew you would be there
Why were you so prominent?
Was it because we had a life before
Were we together in love
Curious yes
But not consumed with the thought
You are the man of my dreams
The way you would hold me
We would be naked while we embraced
Nothing would block the rhythm of our
beating hearts
Pounding against one another
Creating the melody of our love song
Our skin
Like a cashmere blanket
Soft
Warm
You felt so good against me
Slowly dancing to our singsong
Gazing into each other's eyes
No words necessary
It would only disturb the beautiful si-
lence
When I would awaken
Anger filled my mind
Sadness in my heart
However
Somehow I knew you were no fantasy
You were searching for me
And I eagerly but patiently waited

Then
There you were
Fixing the heart of my car
How symbolic
That encounter
Fixed my aching heart
So beautiful you were
When our eyes met
Our souls began to dance
Rejoiced
The ancestors celebrated
The universe responded by parting the
clouds
And the sun shone brightly on our love
Our union was blissful
The I became WE
Joy, happiness, we were complete
Then
We got lost along the way
You no longer smiled so brightly
Laughter left our home
Our home became a house
Joy and happiness no longer resided
Our hearts no longer in sync
The ancestors fell silent
The universe allowed the clouds to
block the sun
Distant
Your heart began to wean from me
And yearn for another
She is where your home was
You did not fuck her
You embraced her
You danced to a new rhythm
Swayed in the sun with her
Penetration was done so gently
Lovingly

Not like me
Forceful
Pounding
Our pelvic area
The only part that touched
My gaze on you
Your eyes on the wall
It ok
What you don't know
Is my time is limited on this plane
I will not take you blatant disrespect
with me
However
I know you love me
Just not the same
I will divulge your secret on my death-
bed
Go ahead and love her
I want you happy
Love her like you once loved me
We will try again in our next life
Goodnight my love
QUIETLY DOES THE SUN SET

§

Lost

Neleh's breathing became heavy, heaving. Where normal breaths used to exist, now only labored. The color in her arms began to turn blue. This was due to the lack of oxygen in her extremities. The body is very unique; it will fight for survival even when demise is imminent.

She had blankets covering the rest of her body, but I can only imagine it was the same for her legs. As I lovingly touched her arm, it was cold. I asked her, "Neleh, are you cold sweetheart? Can I get you more blankets?" She responded to me with a labored "NO." She didn't feel cold at all. The nurse had explained to me she was in a stage called actively dying. She no longer had the need for food or water, she felt neither warm nor cold. However, the one thing she did feel was pain. Was it from the disease, me or a combination of both? I was in agony, unable to help her. Unbearable.

I had to step out of the room, because my tears were uncontrollable and Neleh didn't need that right now. It wasn't about me, but her. My wife's time on this earthly plane was coming to a close, and I am not ready to let her go.

I pulled out my wallet and grabbed her picture out of it. she was beautiful, radiant and full of life. This one is my favorite. The sun was behind her as if it shined on her alone, the wind blew her dress and it made it appear as if she had a train on it. As the waves crashed upon the shore, a white foam formed on them, rolling in one by one. She was barefoot, her toes painted red, her favorite color.

Her hair was pulled back from her face, tucked behind her ears because the wind made it messy and in her way. Just exquisite. Neleh was looking down at a small turtle she found, holding it as if it were her own with utter amazement. It seemed to be amazed with her too, because it was looking up at her. I beheld her beauty. Neleh means "beautiful light." Indeed, I beheld her beauty.

Then our life together began to flash through my mind. All the times I was not there for my wife became the dominant thoughts in my head. Each moment seemed to momentarily pause as if GOD wanted me to face every second of my bad decisions. REMEMBER. I was so filled with grief and regret because I knew I could never make it right. This was a situation I could not fix. There are no flowers I could send, no poems I could write, no romantic dinner date I could set, and no gift I could buy to try to ease the pain she felt every time she called and I did not answer.

Neleh has no use for them now. How could I find such a rare treasure and treat it like fool's gold? I asked the question, but there was no answer.

Not even GOD was talking to me. Sobbing replaced the quiet conversation I had with myself. What a wretch I am, still selfishly thinking of me while she lays there dying. DAMN

I went back into my wife's room, and she opened her eyes and turned toward me. Her gaze followed me to the seat I took next to her bed. I took her hand and began to apologize profusely! I then stood over her and said "I love you with every fiber of my being!" I soaked her face with the wetness of guilt that flowed from my eyes. Neleh gave me a labored smile. For a moment, the love once shared in the beginning of our union came forth.

While we lovingly gazed into each other's eyes, I stroked her jet black hair and fell in love all over again. I was not ready to let her go, I needed more time to try to make it right. I needed to love her past her pain, and I needed to know she could love me past hers. I needed her to live just a lil while longer. I lifted her from the bed, and sat down. I held her fail body as if she were a baby while continuing to stroke her hair.

Fuck! I feel so helpless as a man, as her covering, and as her husband. It was in that moment I truly despised myself! My name, Akachi is a West African name meaning "hand of God" in Igbo. There is someone who will receive judgement, I will live up to my name...

Neleh summoned the strength to speak, using the remaining oxygen in her lungs. Her words are but a whisper, but roared loudly in my ears.

You thought your change in behavior went unnoticed, it didn't. For 10 years, I lay next to you, nothing was hidden from me. I learned the slightest change in your tone. When you, Akachi touched me I felt the difference in pressure, your kisses used to scream I missed you! Now, they are friendly pecks. When we walked together, you no longer walked beside me but in front of me, never looking back to see if I was still there.

When we crossed the street, you no longer held my hand but gave me an open palm. These are just a few things, but I think you get where I am going. What you thought you tucked away in the darkness of your deceit was shining brightly to me. You believed that if you kept to your routine, showered me with gifts and spent time with me that you would go unnoticed. I bet you even patted yourself on the back while looking in the mirror with a Chester cat smile on your face. Silly man.

The rocking suddenly stopped, the tears stopped falling.

I know every time you was with her. I did not need anyone else to come into my home and tell me what my husband was doing. I also know you care for her, genuine feelings. Dare I say love? Her scent permeated through your pores, smelling like an alcoholic that had too much to drink. Foul to me.

At this point, her breathing became more labored.

Akachi begged me to stop talking and just relax (and spare him the agony). I refused! However, I did agree I needed to pause and catch my breath, because I wasn't done. I told him to lay me back in the bed, because I needed to look him in the eyes as I spoke. Reluctantly, Akachi did as I asked.

After laying me down, I told him to press the call button and request a nasal cannula, because I needed my mouth free to continue this conversation. Once again, without a moment of hesitation he did what I asked of him, but inside I knew he was in agony! He was not ready for what else I had to say!

I told my husband I appreciated the effort to leave her at the threshold, but it was unsuccessful. I also told him every time he got in our bed, it felt like there was a third person in the bed with us. I never agreed to a ménage a trios!

The look on his face was one for the books, the pain that was visible saddened me inside. Although he was so wrong for what he had done, he was still my husband, and I still love him. However, that would not stop me from continuing to divulge his secrets!

Believe me, it hurts inside, I know my demise is near and will end the chapter of us before he feels its time. I was not ready to leave, not ready to give up on us, not ready to acknowledge I never held life within my womb, our legacy together in the flesh. I am ready now. I have made my peace with everyone I ever loved, and now make peace with the man I dedicated my life to before I say goodnight.

Akachi asked with a shaky voice, tears filling his eyes again "why did you stay?" "Why did you put up with that?" I told him, "my vows and my word is bond." I loved you past your indiscretion, past my own sorrow and past your selfishness. For better or worse, right? I forgave you long ago, and regardless of what you've done, I know you still love me. And that, gave me the strength to hold on. Now, my grip has to loosen, I have to let you go, and you must do the same."

Now listen closely my love, I don't have much time left. His eyes became wide, bulging out of his head. Akachi stood up, began to softly protest, curse the universe itself and defiantly declare I was not going anywhere yet. My poor husband. He knows he can never make it right; he knows this isn't something he can throw a checkbook at. He was not the one in control; no prayer he could utter would change the inevitable. I am going. I am going to have an endless sleep. ALONE.

I told him to have a seat, and take my hand. My request was granted. I began my final instruction to him.

My love, it was destined for you to meet her, become intimate and even fall in love. I love you deeply enough to release you. I release the guilt that you are feeling and approve of your new life with her.

WHAT THE FUCK?! I cannot believe my wife is telling me to continue this affair!

Now I know what you are thinking my darling husband, and this will no longer be an affair, because I will be gone.

I can't close my mouth; I cannot come to grips with this! I cannot utter a word, because I am in COMPLETE shock!

My husband listened intently, his tears streamed down his face even more.

Love like this is what you read about, I never thought I would experience it in my lifetime! She is an amazing woman, indeed. To love me so deeply...SIGH

I will take the untainted part of your love with me. I will forever love you beyond my last breath in this vessel. I will find you in my next life, do not fret, our souls will recognize one another. I don't know when your time will come, but I promise in our next chapter of our lives our souls will recognize one another. I promise. Look for the woman with the lotus blossom in her hair. This will be a sign to you. Your mind will have to process this, but your heart will already know. In the meantime, love this woman as she loves you. My ancestors who are coming for me already showed her to me. She is beautiful.

Not nearly as beautiful and radiant as you, my love! There is not another being alive that can compare to you! I hate myself for the love I felt for her!

Now now baby, it's ok. Remember its ok to love her, do not withdraw from her because I will be gone. Allow her to comfort you, you will need it. Those broken pieces of your heart, she will help you put them back together.

She can do no such thing!

Yes, she can. However, it will not be a heart for me. I can't be! Live my love, I release you, because I will not carry this part of our life with me. I will not take with me ANY pain!

Neleh's time to drift away now settling, she placed her other hand on mine and said she suffers not. It was as if she was passing her peace on to me. I relaxed just a little. My tears began to slowly drip. I placed my hand on her heart, it was erratically beating. Her breaths became very slow. I knew it was time.

With the last bit of air in her lungs, she said I love you beyond my last breath, and I will take your love with me on this new journey I am about to experience! Now release me my husband. Release me. I told her; there is no greater love than the love of our Creator, and I know your ancestors are at the door to the light to take you home. I will always love you and I promise to find you again, my LOTUS GODDESS. Now go my love, walk into the light and enjoy the peace and love from those before me. I LOVE YOU! I release you.

With that, she closed her eyes and was unable to speak again. Her breathing became extremely labored, only taking a breath every minute. There were gurgling sounds that accompanied the shallow breaths, which nauseated me! I wanted to call for the doctor, but I knew there was a DNR in place, and all they could do was stand by until it was over.

This was nothing like you see in the movies. Because of that deception, I expected something angelic and beautiful. This was nothing of the sort! The agony, anxiety and fear that took hold of me was beyond what I could mortally stand! DAMN THAT DNR! The ordeal felt like an eternity! I took my wife's hand and begged her to let the vessel go, it's no good to her anymore. PLEASE!

Neleh let out one long exhale. Her body went limp and she was gone. That, was the final exchange between oxygen and carbon dioxide within her lungs. The last breath, the last time her chest would rise and fall, and the last time for…anything. She was gone!

I began to cry as loudly as I could! The doctor and nurses rushed into the room, and seemed to split into two teams. One to make sure she was deceased and call the time of death, and the other to make sure I would not pass out from shock! I told them I was ok, let me near my wife and thanked them for all they had done for my beloved.

I stroked her hair with one hand, and took her lifeless hand into my other. I leaned down, told her goodnight my Lotus Goddess, kissed her on her forehead, gently rubbed her hand, placed it on her chest and walked out of the room. How am I supposing to do as she asked of me? How can I continue to love that woman? I now realize, not only do I despise myself for the pain I inflicted on my wife, but now there is enmity between me and THAT WOMAN! She will know what I feel shortly…

Love Lost

After I walked out of the place where
your soul departed this earth
I looked to the sky
It was a mixture of sun and clouds
The clouds were grey and full
I closed my eyes
Put my head back
I took a deep breath to inhale the
fresh air
Just then

It began to rain
The sun still shone brightly in the sky
Tears began to roll down my face
But the rain camouflaged them perfectly
Oh how you loved sun showers!
Are you speaking to me my love?
This rain feels warm
Different
The sun's rays are especially warm
Are you sending me love baby?
My heart flutters with excitement
There are butterflies in my stomach
Of course you are speaking to me
Transcendence
It must be a beautiful experience
You kept your word my love
And took my untainted part of love with
you
This rain
As it washes over me
I can feel the peace that you desired
for me to have
You, my departed wife
So selfless
Even in your final hour
You are the woman spoken highly of in
the bible
The Virtuous One
Even with those well versed words
It cannot encompass everything you were
I did not deserve love so deep
However
You gave it without question
My LOTUS GODDESS
You walk among the Gods
And have become one yourself
Yet

You will leave endless paradise
Just to be with me again
There is no greater love
I love you with everything I got
And dig into the reserves when I feel
there isn't enough
However
You must forgive me my wife
I will not grant your request
I will not love that woman anymore
What you did not know
She is with child
I am so sorry
I despise that fact
I will not love that kid
That is not a part of our legacy
I will not love her
That is a fact
You knew I was not ready to let you go
Not ready to end our chapter
I forgive
You told me at the end
When there was nothing more that could
be done
Or was there?
Did I hurt you so deeply?
That you gave up?
No matter
This heart is for you
I have reclaimed it from her
And this world
I will ask you when I see you again
Just out of curiosity of course
Nothing you will say will change a
thing
You are my love
My body was elsewhere

But my heart was in our home
In you
Once again
Forgive me my love
I am not ready to sleep alone
I will fix that
And I reject your peace

§

Neleh was just as beautiful in
death as she was in life. The mortician
was able to restore her to their most
glorious moment, the day they married.
Her shiny jet black hair was pulled up
into a bun; her diamond headpiece was
like a net that cascaded from the front
of her bun to just between her eye-
brows. Her make-up was flawless, eye-
brows perfectly arched, her skin had a
light bronze-like glow, eyelashes
curled and her lips were painted with a
beautiful shade of red.

She was dressed in her Swarovski
encrusted crystal and lace wedding
gown. Her manicured hands were crossed,
resting gently on her chest, as if she
were holding her heart. I specifically
made that request. Flawless, endless
beauty graced that church that day. She
looked as if she were sleeping.

I spared no expense to make sure
she was laid to rest with elegance and
grace. The casket was gold, with pearl
handles. On the corners were pearl
cherubs, there to carry her spirit

to heaven. The casket shown like the sun every time light hit and illuminated the church even more than it was. My favorite picture of her adorned the top, and the inside was lined with the purest of white cushioning I could find. There were flowers sent from all over, so many the church could barely fit them all in. She was like a beautiful sunny day in an arboretum, and I did everything to resemble such an atmosphere within 4 walls.

The choir sang with such power, it vibrated your very bones. I thought they were going to literally blow the roof off the building! She was truly loved by all! God's presence was certainly welcomed into this place, except by me. I felt an anger boiling up inside me as the rest of the attendees felt the fruits of the Spirit.

People got up after the song was over and while filled with Love, approached the front of the church to give a kind word, tell a story, or just to proclaim the Love they have for her for all time. Those who could complete their thought without a breakdown extended their condolences and wish for peace to the family.

After the Pastor lovingly delivered his sermon, all in attendance had their final viewing, said their tearful goodbyes. Her broken hearted family and friends entered their cars,
and began the procession to her final resting place. After one last prayer,

she was lowered into the ground, and
everyone proceeded to the repass. But
not me, I could not bear to see
anyone who would remotely resemble my
beloved. I returned home.

§

Akachi couldn't live, not without
his soul. He watched his universe, his
life, his love return to the dirt from
which she came.
The sun was out, but his world was
dark. The birds were chirping, but to
him there was silence. He was in limbo,
a place where there was vast emptiness.
Silence. The sun was out along with the
clouds and the rain. Man, how she loved
sun showers. This phenomenon was a
beautiful experience they shared, it
seemed to wash away all the dirty se-
crets, the negativity of the world, and
help life come forth from the earth.
Now, the showers didn't seem to wash
away anything. Instead, each raindrop
that hit his skin was cold, the sound
was like quiet weeping. The misery of
the world manifested in the form of
falling water.
Akachi turned the doorknob without
resistance. He realized he never locked
the door, nor did he care. This was a
house, never again to be a home. It
held no value to him anymore. After he
entered the house, he walked through
the living room passing the dirty
clothes, liquor bottles and the food

that began to rot because he ordered but did not eat what he spent his money on. The smell of funk hit his nostrils and he winced a second.

Recovering quickly from the assault on his nose, he picked up the bottle of brown liquor off the coffee table he had not consumed yet. Twisting off the cap, he then turned the bottle straight up to his lips and took a continuous gulp until he had to stop for air. He resumed his walk through the living room until he reached a dark corner. Akachi put his back against the wall, and slid down until he was in a sitting position. With his legs stretched out, bottle in hand and darkness as his friend, there he sat.

He couldn't keep his mind clear of the end, the demise of his beloved Neleh. Endless images of her flashed through his mind. The affair he had no longer brought him deceptive joy. Now, the emotions Akachi felt for the other woman turned to unforgiveable guilt. So consumed with these thoughts, it was as if he was in a stupor. Stuck in one spot, he was unable to move. Paralyzed.

Silent tears flowed from his blood shot and swollen eyes. The phone rang, but he ignored it. Text messages came in a flurry, lighting up his cell also ignored. The sun set, and night had fallen. It was then he finally blinked his eyes and looked around. Darkness about, he welcomed it. This, is where he is most comfortable. He

rose from the corner he found himself
in, adjusted his clothing, took a deep
breath, and made his resolve.

§

The showers earlier had turned
into a mild storm. Now, the cold
raindrops were accompanied by the sound
of rumbling thunder. Lightening danced
across the sky, temporarily brightening
the darkness of the sky. This was a
perfect atmospheric setting, because
madness has finally taken its hold on
me.

I began to have a conversation
with death himself, telling him he will
not win. He will not separate me from
my once in a lifetime love! There was a
response to my defiant statement. It
said; "what are you going to do about
it?" with a sinister laugh. I spun
around, searching the corners of the
room in the dark. Nothing. However,
with a sinister laugh of my own, I re-
sponded "I will show you what I can do.
I will go into the afterlife and find
my wife!"

After that, I found myself running
down to the basement and grabbed the
shovel. I was holding it in both hands,
stared at it wide-eyed, breathing heavy
and sweating. Between clenched teeth, I
made a declaration to the universe it-
self and said "tonight, I will be reu-
nited with my wife!" After that, I ran

upstairs, went out the front door without bothering to close it to my car parked in the driveway.

I looked up into the night sky, rain heavily hitting my face, and let an insidious smile creep across my face. I, Akachi silently challenged GOD himself to stop me from what I was about to do. Nothing huh? I thought so! I then threw the shovel in the front seat, got in the car and turned the ignition. It stalled, which immediately infuriated me. I began to yell obscenities at Death, the Creator and all the heavenly hosts shouting "you mutha fuckas will not stop me!" I turned the key again, and the car started. Throwing the car in gear, I sped off into the stormy night to accomplish my mission.

§

He reached the cemetery, but it was locked so he couldn't drive to the place where his destiny was laid to rest. The gate was too high to jump over, and the space between the bars was too narrow to squeeze in-between. Laughing out loud, Akachi said "IS THIS THE BEST YOU GOT ASSHOLE?!" He looked to the right and studied the stone wall. Then he got an idea…

He got back into his car and pulled it up to the wall. It was so close that the front bumper made contact. He got out, threw the shovel over the wall and climbed on top of the hood. He jumped up, gripped the top of the wall and pulled himself up. He threw his left leg up and swung his body over the wall. Not caring what he landed on, he fell over and landed on his feet at first.

He lost his balance and fell. Pain shot from his ankle straight up to his brain. It appeared as if he sprained his ankle. Laughing again, he didn't care. Pain was a delicious staple in his life, and he ate it as if it was the breakfast of the champions. He stood, tightened the strings on his boot and proceeded to limp to the grave.

Once he reached the spot, he stood there for a moment. The red and white roses were still in place, along with the ribbon that read "LOVING WIFE, DAUGHTER AND FRIEND TO ALL." The foot-prints left behind from those that at-tended the service were washed away. The dirt now muddy and soft, it began to sink in that this was her final place. She will no longer jog along the river, go shopping with her girl-friends, dance the night away in his arms!

The most devastating reality is she will never know what it feels like to hold life within her womb. They will never be able to begin a family. More tears began to escape his eyes and blended with the rain that fell from the sky. It was then in that moment that he remembered the other woman was pregnant with his seed. This thought did not bring him an ounce of pleasure. Instead, rage filled his heart and rose to his mind. HOW DARE THAT BITCH BE ABLE TO CARRY THE BABY MY WIFE SHOULD HAVE HAD! HMMM…it seems there is something else that must be done before I greet my wife…

He politely excused himself from the presence of his wife, telling her he would return soon, don't fret or be angry with him. He began to quickly walk back to his car. The rage the bubbled through his veins was so intense he walked almost normally, not feeling a thing.

He reached the wall, but realized it was too high to just jump up and reach the top. Then he looked down and seen he was still holding the shovel. The shovel was the type that was wide, and had a handle on it. Good shit! He put the handle end into the dirt and leaned it against the wall. He then stepped up onto the top, and it was enough for him to reach the top of the wall. He did the same thing, this time more careful of how he landed. Another sharp pain shot from his ankle. He winced, and ignored it. He got back into his car and drove to the source of his rage. This fire will be quenched.

He looked around for something that would mark the spot that he was in, so when he returned, he would be able to recover the shovel. He found a big, oddly shaped rock. He then picked it up and placed it in the spot where he wanted it. He jumped in his car, and this time it started without hesitation. He put it in reverse, then drive and sped to the source of his contention.

Once he arrived at her house, he realized he must look a mess! Looking into the rear view mirror, this suspicion was confirmed. He said to himself; "she would never let me in looking like this." Then it seemed that same voice responded saying; "change that look of rage into one of despair. You did just bury your wife." He then nodded his head in agreement (he was not on the brink of insanity, he jumped right into it!) and said "I will tell her I was walking around in the rain trying to clear my head." Perfect.

Oh shit! The mud on my boots will leave footprints behind, and I know my ankle has to have support to keep it stable. DAMN! The voice answered "remove the boots when you walk in, the rain will get rid of any trace of an imprint." Thank you voice of reason or Death, you're not so bad after all! "Don't forget to wipe the place clean, and make sure no one sees you entering her house!" He responded; "why? I see you doubt my declaration, no matter now." He has danced around the burning embers with demons, the crackling of the fire creating its own singsong. He has married into insanity…

Getting out of the car, I take one more look into the side mirror to be sure I have the face of the one I have to put forward, despair. I need no other weapon but my bare hands. This is personal. I could not stop thinking to myself; "I want to feel the hyoid bone break in her neck, stare into her eyes as the veins fill with blood and bulge from her sockets, and watch her gasp for air." Oh, and "not before breaking the bones in her body with every blow, and stomping the baby, blood and guts out of her beaten and bruised body."

The enmity I feel for that woman is nothing like this world has ever known.

My wife died with the knowledge of her existence. She knew my hands not only caressed her body, but hers too. My wife had to live out her last days knowing that I made love to another, I placed my dick into another and loved the way her pussy invited me into her! Consumed with the blame all on her, and none for himself, he walked to the door and rang the bell. When she opened the door, he greeted her with "*hello Clarisse...*"

§

Nicole

Nicole was surprised by the visit because she knew where he was. She had placed many calls to his cell, along with text messages that went without a response. She instinctively rubbed her stomach, and took his hand. Sorrow was written across Akachi's face, and Nicole knew the end had finally come.

Secretly, she was filled with joy, because now she was no longer number two. They could finally be happy, and bring their legacy of their passion and love into the world without disruption. She could finally have her man, emerge from the shadows and proudly walk among the rest of the world by his side. So caught up in the moment with her thoughts, she had not realized he did not call her by her name or fully understand the reference to that name...

"Oh sweetheart, I am so sorry for your loss!" Nicole stepped forward and wrapped her hands around his neck, slightly going up on her tip toes. He held her around her waist, but that isn't where he wanted his hands to be. A greedy smirk went across her face. What she didn't realize is that one crossed his as well. After she let go of the embrace, she gazed lovingly into Akachi's eyes for a moment, and invited him in from the rain.

Taking his hand, she led the man of her dreams into the sanctity of her home. A home she was now happy to give up, and move in with her future. Little did she realize, this was no longer the man she loved, cherished, and adored.

This man danced with the demons of despair, rage and murder. He loved every minute of it! Akachi took off his boots at the door, and practically salivated at the mouth because of what was about to happen. Nicole went into the kitchen to put a pot of hot water on for his favorite tea. As she was preparing the drink, she began to ask questions about the demise of her rival. This was not out of concern, but sheer and utter delight for herself.

Honey, was she at peace when the moment came?

Yes.

Was she in any pain? (I hope that bitch felt every bit of pain!) I hope they were able to make her as comfortable as possible. (NOT lol)

Yes, she had something for the pain. (I know you don't really care you despicable bitch!)

Did you hold her hand? (If he held her hand, I swear I will sanitize the shit out of it! She thought to herself...)

Of course.

I heard they are not coherent when they are at that stage. Did she know who you were?

Yes, and yes. I don't want to talk about it anymore.

My apologies. Ok my love that is enough.

I danced for joy on the inside. It didn't matter if he wanted to talk about it or not. I have a friend who works at the hospital where she was. I will get the juicy details from her later. A necessary call will be made to her as soon as he leaves the house!

Akachi went into the living room and sat on the plush, butter soft leather sofa. I know he hates the feel of my sofa! He is a more of a hard leather type, and I will be sure to buy that furniture when we move into our new place!

But he was thinking; "I hate this hard leather sofa! However, that wouldn't matter anymore in a few minutes."

He had one leg crossed and resting just above the knee, and with his arms stretched out on the sofa he stared at me in the kitchen preparing his tea. I acted like I didn't notice at first. He is so handsome! So, after a minute or two, I caught his stare, smiled back at him then continued my task.

§

"I hate that bastard she is carrying! I never realized how much of a daughter of an ugly bitch she is! Sleeping with a married man, trying to bare his child, she disgusts me and I cannot wait to end their miserable life!" All of these thoughts hidden behind my sorrowful face, a true monster was certainly born, and I loved every second of this feeling!

Here you go honey, piping hot just like you like it. See, I know what you like, I pay attention to what you love and have no problems granting your every desire to ensure your happiness!

Thank you, sweetheart.

He took a sip of his tea, savored the flavor and told me it was made to order. He placed the cup back on the saucer, stared into the tea cup, and while never looking up he said; "however, my wife made it to perfection." His tone of voice was monotone, empty and meant to sting. After saying that, he slowly looked up, slightly tilted and turned his head towards me, and let his eyes tell the utter disgust he felt for me!

I glared at him, growling through clenched teeth, I said; "YOU BASTARD! I have been very patient with you, listening to your sorry stories about what's going on in your home, her illness and how it was exhausting you! I have waited on you hand and foot, inhaled the funky scent of that woman ALL over your clothes and STILL allowed you to touch me and lay in my bed! The stench of that hospital permeates from your clothing, and you have the audacity to bring that shit into MY home?! FUCK YOU YOU SON OF AN UGLY BITCH! I AM SICK AND TIRED OF YOU AND EVERYTHING YOU BRING!"

Standing up and adjusting his clothing he asked her "are you done?' Did you get all you needed out of your system?" If not, I will have a seat and allow you to finish your rant. Obviously, you held this for some time.

FUCK YOU ASSHOLE!

Humph, I guess you're done. He calmly walked across the room to retrieve the remote to the stereo system. He pressed play, and Sade's sultry voice bellowed out of the BOSE speakers.

Don't you try to bring me down from this! It won't work; I am so fuckin pissed with you!

I'm not.

He turned the volume up, knowing the neighbors were used to her listening to this song at such a high tone. She had her back to him, so she didn't know he was quietly putting his gloves on. Before approaching her, he dimmed the lights. Strangely he wanted a serene atmosphere as he took the life from her. I am not a complete monster; I will send her to hell comfortably.

Stop playin godammit, I'm so mad at you right now.

Silence.

When Nicole finally turned around, Akachi punched her in the face. She spun and fell back on the sofa. Her eyes wide, she couldn't believe he actually put his hands on her! He hit her so hard her jaw dislocated, so speaking was not an option. Without uttering a word, he continued to pummel her and her unborn child with a rage not rivaled by anyone.

All she could do was ball up and try in vain to protect her child. Tears of regret, fear and impending doom flowed down her face. He didn't care, not even for a millisecond! He put his hands around her throat and squeezed with all of his might. Gasping for air and clawing at his arms she fought for their lives. Blood vessels began to burst in her eyes, and he savored every moment. When she realized it was hopeless, she said a prayer asking for forgiveness, and told her baby she will see him on the other side.

Yes, it was a boy. Her hyoid bone snapped, and it was over.

Goodnight

I thought he and I would have forever
But I was wrong
I loved him with everything I had
And when I felt it wasn't enough
I dug into my reserves and found a reservoir of blissfulness
If I had to describe it
A cascading waterfall over a cliff
The sun glistening
Reflecting off of the water
The mist held rainbows
The rushing waters sang a song
He told me he loved me
Showed me the many facets of Love
Moonlit walks

Cuddles in the dimmed light
Tight embraces while he deeply stroked
my honey pot
Kisses on the forehead while he stroked
my hair
Together
We made a beautiful thing
LIFE
We would be a family
One that didn't have to be hidden
No whispers in the night
No hiding by day
But I was wrong
There will be a forever
An eternity I suppose
But not with who I thought
Never believed for a second
His love would turn on me
On US
The cascading waters turned to lava
The beautiful sun blocked by the dark
clouds
The only light is from the destructive
fire
Absolute carnage in its flowing wake
I am sorry my child
I was wrong
I didn't notice the venom in his tone
Paid no attention to the rage spilling
over into his embrace
My child
I will continue to hold you in my arms
You will always find Love with me
We will face eternity together
GOODNIGHT MY HEARTBEAT

He decided there was no need to
clean up any trace of him, because he
would not be around to face any conse-
quences. He looked around the room, no-
ticed there was blood splatter all over
the walls and the furniture that lay
broken all over the living room. A lamp
knocked off the end table on the floor
struggled to remain lit. You could hear
a buzzing sound as it flashed on and
off. Akachi felt proud of his work.
Yes, he embraced the demons he now
called friends. Insanity absolute. He
walked over to her lifeless body and
gave her one final kick in the stomach.

Nicole, you will ever see the
light of day again. Neither of you de-
serve to. Sorry kid, blame your bitch
of a mother for never taking your first
breath outside of that wretched womb.

I got back in my car, and took a
moment to catch my breath. The deed is
done, and I feel SO fuckin good right
now! Now it's time to be with you my
love, I'm coming! I left my rage behind
in that house, so there is no need to
speed. The last leg of my journey is
underway, I can't contain the smile
forming on my face! I plan on smiling
the entire ride back to what will be-
come my new home with the love of my
life.

Repeating the steps as before, he
went over the wall and back to the hole
he dug. This time, it was not raining.
It seemed to stop after he committed
the heinous crime of ending the lives

of his mistress and HER unborn child. Baby, you must be pleased with the outcome, because you lament no more! I'm sorry it took some time for me to return, but I am here as I promised.

The sinister voice spoke and said "Good job my guy! And you were right, no need to clean up."

Shut up, I don't need you to chime in anymore.

Akachi opened the casket, and found Neleh in the same position he left her in. Smiling, he remembered that's the way it was when he would leave at night. When he returned, she would still be in the same position, sleeping peacefully.

He carefully let himself down in to the grave, careful not to step on her in the coffin. He positioned himself beside her, put his arm under her head and fixed her hair with his other hand so it wouldn't pull.

You're so cold baby, I am sorry I didn't think to bring you your favorite blanket. I know you hate to be cold. He fell silent, just taking in her beauty. He became slightly disturbed because she didn't open her eyes. He remembered then, she was not on this plane. Don't worry my love; you will not be alone anymore. I'm coming!

Before entering the grave, he took out a bottle of opioids, OxyContin to be precise. These were left behind by his wife. He ingested the entire bottle. The effects of taking the overdose began to settle in. He resisted the urge to throw it back up, because he wanted no chance of remaining in this world. His heart began to beat erratically, and he felt very dizzy. At this time, he mumbled goodbye world, and fuck you. My darling, here I come. He closed the casket, held her close and began his journey back to the one he loves.

Wait a fuckin minute! If she knew what I was doing, then why did she sleep so peacefully?!

DAMN, TOUCHE!

The next day, the groundskeeper found the grave had been opened. Out of curiosity, he opened the casket. Inside, he found a well preserved beautiful woman, and a bloated, discolored man beside her. The stench of bodily fluids and decomposition almost knocked him out. He knew who he was, and about the affair he had. He was his cousin. Shaking his head, he said "in life and even in death he desecrated her, the place where she laid her head for all time."

I am so blessed to have had the chance to love such a beautiful woman.

Yes, my darling, and continue to love me you shall.

Twin sister Neveah, you played your role well, Salute and Goodnight.

Mark held my secret with ease, he never threatened to disclose any details of my plan to be free of that man! Many men say they love you, but he certainly proved it, at least up to this point. This is heavy, and I certainly do not feel as strongly as I did while I was putting this together. Actually, I think I would rather be free to explore...in the meantime, I need to touch him in the place that will keep him wrapped around my finger. Time for some action! Mark, my darling...

The Thick Juice Box

Push me beyond limits set by man
Make me beg for mercy
I do not wish for you to grant
Twist me
Choke me
Pound me
Spread me
I will fight you
Disobedience
You must punish me
I've been a bad girl
Naughty
Tease me
Taunt me
Delve into me
Appetence-Seek
Blindfold-Dark
Senses heightened
Confining binds
Restrained
Ball gag

Red
Silence Speechless
Hot wax
Heated
Burning
Cold cherry
Iced
The pudenda muscles strong
Pink caverns Hot
I've popped my cherry
Dripping
Sweet
Succulent
I AM THE THICK JUICE BOX
Quench your thirst
Sooth your throat
Lap it up
Flick your tongue
Ravenous
My body is writhing
Back arching
Squirming Twitching
I push my SHE in his face
Fuckin his mouth
Sweating
Throbbing Pulsating
Rhythm Erratic
Pussy lips full
Clit hard
She has come out to play
Engulf
FEAST SUCK
OH SHIT
Ignition
MAKE ME ORGASM
Earth shattering
Detonation

Combustion
Liquid sweetness
Expulsion
NO
Torment
Torture
Excruciating
Anguish
Manipulation Mental
I AM THE THICK JUICE BOX
Poke the hole
Vibrator
PENETRATE MY SHE
Simultaneous
Indulge
Go deep Hit my bottom
OH YES
GRIPPING THE D
SPANKING MY ASS
QUAKING TREMBLING
UNCONTROLLED CONVULSING
SCREAMING
RELEASING
Synchronous
Safety word
MANGOS...

She thinks this is my first experience huh? Funny. I am more than happy to play the love-struck, simple minded man she now believes I am. Her own ego gets in her way. It has not occurred to her that I contributed to the plan. That smugness...birds of a feather do flock together! Yes, Neleh this most definitely IS about to get interesting, indeed.

DARK FANTASY

DARK LOVE the fallen need love too

People always want power, and some be-
come so obsessed with it that they will
do anything to obtain it. But what's
usually not remembered, is things that
are borrowed MUST be repaid... These two
dark spirits are invoked to deal with
the unruly. They feed off of fear and
provoke nightmares. Madness and insan-
ity are sure to come. However, this is
pleasurable pain to some, (until they
realize there is no end to it) horror
and torment to others. Demise is inevi-
table. However, what happens when
these two powerful beings meet? Please
enjoy a glimpse into the world of Dark
Fantasy. Meet Queen Khalidah and King
Yashe.

QUEEN KHALIDAH

Who exactly am I
I AM THE WOMAN OF PLEASURE/ETERNAL
HURTING
Are you ready to look within my mind?
Be prepared for what I wonder
Make your resolve now
To not be afraid
You may find this is what you want
Addictive
I go beyond mortal thoughts
Superseded what the human body can han-
dle
You raise an eyebrow
Curiosity engaged
Your desires taken to heights unknown

The lustful beast within
No longer restrained
Limits not granted
There is no safety word
I will set every nerve on fire
Senses ignited at once
The pleasurable pain I will inflict
Will cause dopamine to burst forth
Euphoric waves
Control lost
Visions of me will dance within
Certain sounds
Will cause uncontrolled throbbing
My scent in the air
Will invoke spontaneous eruptions
Intoxication achieved
Dare to come close
Will you?
To some I am known as Darkness
To some I am the Light
I am the key to open Pandora's Box
Never afraid of what I find
I have Power beyond the Spirits
They consult me for knowledge
A goddess is the rumor
Because my origins are unknown
Many have tried to find my roots with-
out success
Weaknesses are unknown
The evilest fetish is child's play to
Khalidah
There has been nothing of interest
I have a job to do and nothing more
My level of wealth is beyond what the
eye can see
No figure can be given

Wealth beyond the Arabs and entire con-
tinents
Who can ignore the call of the banshee?
The siren calls of the succubus
Once you have been in my presence
Once I have deposited my essence into
you
If I chooses to summon you, I will sum-
mon you
Some will quiver with excitement
Others for different reasons like Fear
My name invokes nightmares
Beautiful Terror
Obey me you must and cease all activity
Make excuses to your family
Walk away from me?
TRY
Return you *will*
Return to the place when heaven and
hell collaborate
Resistance is futile
To the one who has found hidden
strength
I make this declaration to you
THAT
Is a fatal choice

§

KING YASHE

To some I am living darkness
Fear
To others
I am the answer to a forbidden request
Once I have been summoned
The path will vanish
Forgiveness not granted
Pleas fall from the mouth
Into vastness
Empty space
I am the Alpha and Omega
Of despair
I command the wicked
The tormentors on earth
And beyond
My origin unknown
My true name unpronounceable
With the human tongue
It is not wise to step into the beyond
Research any curiosity
Your end will not come swiftly
Guaranteed to drive you
Into madness
Insomnia
Schizophrenia
I have no weakness
A god killing weapon
A mere mortal
Flesh Bones Blood
I feed to my beasts
The most dire
Evil Grotesque Violent
Gruesome thought
Your simple mind can conjure

Is but child's play to me
Wealth is an infinite reality
I have no need for rest
This thing you call joy
Is when I am spilling fresh blood
I mutilate for sheer pleasure
The sound of crushing bones
Climactic
I have the power to hold your beating
heart
Squeeze
Feast
And keep you alive
Shrieking
Screaming
Agony
Pain
Powers me
You will beg for death
Hell will suffice
Anything to be released from my grasp
I will not grant you release
My appearance is deceiving
This undesirable flesh
Hides my secret
I am whoever you desire
Your dream comes true
When I hear your desperate call
Those thoughts that lie in the dark
crevasse of your mind
The recess of your heart
Once I have implanted my seed
You will give birth to madness
Insanity
I will summon you as I please
Some will shudder with excitement
Others for different reasons

Nightmare Terror Torment
That beauty is in the eye of the be-
holder
My name invokes nightmares
Welcomed
Rejected
Obey you must
All activity shall end
Seek me, Run away
All paths lead to me
Escape elusive
Resistance futile
When my wings spread
Your demise imminent
The one who would dare challenge me
Mortality is meaningless...

§

...after King Yashe summoned the beats of
Hell to come and remove his victim from
his presence into eternal night, he
sensed something different in the air.
As the wind blew. He was able to actu-
ally *taste* her after he flicked his
tongue out of his mouth, the same as a
snake searching for prey. He deeply in-
haled and became intoxicated, felt eu-
phoric and was stimulated. His wings
expanded, his chest bulged forward, and
every muscle tensed to the point of
pain, which he savored. *What is this*

feeling? I have never known such a thing, especially not on this planet!

He had to contain himself, because his true form was a large as the tallest mountain known to man. That form could only be handled in another dimension. One he was not ready to return to, because after all, he enjoyed inflicting trepidation on "God's creation." Laughable. Although fear was NOT a part of his being, he was not ready to crush the Earth just yet.

Queen Khalidah, I am sorry! I should have never tried to seek out a way to destroy you! PLEASE! He begged as she walked slowly towards him. I have no use for your sorrow, and will not grant you once ounce of pity. You knew what you were doing, this didn't happen in a second.

Meticulous and calculated, you took time to do this. I told you, I have no weakness and cannot be destroyed. The same cannot be said for you, disgusting creature. I despise the very existence of your kind, "God's creation." Laughable.

So frail, and yet your kind believes you are the strongest among the true beings of the Universe. Now, (she extended out her arm with fingers straight) your nightmare begins! She made a tight fist, and with that the bones in his body was crushed all at once.

Just then, she sensed something she never had before. Her victim was screaming (because she didn't let him die) and she needed to concentrate. So, she took his voice and focused on this sensation that vibrated throughout her body. She was immediately aroused! Her wings expanded, her breasts became full, her nipples hardened, and there was a pulsating between her thighs that she never felt before! She began to touch herself, first in her newly-discovered erogenous zone with one hand, and pinched her nipples with the other. *"WHAT IS THIS?!"* the Queen thought to herself…

The King, full of eroticism flowing through him, was following the scent to his curiosity. For the first time, he did not intend to kill, but to explore. She summoned her faithful minions to remove the rotting meat from her presence so she could follow *desire* to its lair.

Entranced they both were by these newly discovered sensations, they literally bumped into each other as they turned the corner. Their eyes met with an intense passion, chests heaving, the intense heat melting metal like flowing water. He spoke first, "may I explore you?" After a bit of the shock wore off, she responded in a deep sultry voice; "that would remain to be seen, I will give you the chance to make your resolve. I see your confidence just might be the cause of the fall of your empire…"

Yes, you are right, that would remain to be seen, I love that you already underestimate a King...

THANK YOU

If you made it to this page, then I hope you thoroughly enjoyed the emotional rollercoaster I meant for you to ride! I hope I did not leave you in a dismal mood, and you will eagerly await the next installment! I assure you the next will not disappoint! My aim is to do something different from other authors. I wanted to publish a genre-bending book. What I mean is I wanted there to be a variety of stories, poems and genres in a single book, and flow together like a couple dancing in perfect rhythm to a pulsating beat. I wanted to take you, on a literary adventure! Once again, my goal is to ignite your imagination, make you feel as if you were there, and connect with the characters as if you knew them personally! Please feel free to spread the word with anyone of your choosing, and visit my social media pages or email me. I thank you from the depths of me for reading! I hope I have made a new fan! Stay close and stay tuned for updates on book signings, spoken word performances and other events. Peace and manty blessings!

Author
MzSHE